The Matinée Murders

A Provincetown Mystery

Jeannette de Beauvoir

HOMEPORT
PRESS

The Matinée Murders: A Provincetown Mystery
Copyright © 2020 by Jeannette de Beauvoir

Published by HomePort Press
PO Box 1508
Provincetown, MA 02657
www.HomePortPress.com

ISBN   978-1-7340533-3-3
eISBN 978-1-7340533-4-0

Cover Design by Miladinka Milic

The Matinée Murders is a work of fiction. Other than those individuals who have given their permission and certain well-known landmarks, all names, characters, places, situations, and incidents are the products of the author's imagination and used fictitiously. Any other resemblance to actual events, or persons, living or dead, is purely coincidental.

Also by
Jeannette de Beauvoir

1

N o one is a movie star forever," the voice on the television was saying as I pulled my reheated rice and beans from the microwave. "At some point, you find it's time to move on."

"Say it isn't so," I muttered, balancing the dish and a glass of Côtes du Rhône as I made my way back to the sofa and managed to put everything on the coffee table without spillage. Another triumph of poise and grace, thank you very much. On the TV, actor and heartthrob Brett Falcone was still talking. "And you have to understand, it goes deeper than that. There's this kind of leading-man role these days—you could plug any of us into, it doesn't really matter who it is, you know? Any one of us, given that same role, would get the same result." He paused significantly and looked directly at the camera. "So I'm stepping back from all that."

Sure you are. Ibsen jumped up next to me and started purring, anticipating sharing in the evening's repast. I pushed him away and took a sip of wine, pressing pause on the remote.

I was watching the interview with Brett Falcone—I still couldn't bring myself to think of him as just "Brett," even though he'd told me to—not because I was a particular fan, though I suppose in some ways I was. Anyone who's been to the movies in the past decade has seen and enjoyed his handsome bad-boy persona dozens of times.

But this was more personal. I'm the wedding planner at the Race Point Inn in Provincetown, and Brett—there, I did it!—was coming here to get married. Next *week*. It was enough to send Mike, the inn's manager, close to swooning.

It wasn't as if we didn't already have a lot going on. We were fast approaching the first day of the Provincetown International Film Festival, and as usual the inn was hosting a plethora of parties and events for attendees and donors. Adrienne the diva chef was flatout, Mike was downing espressos like they were going out of style, and Glenn, the inn's owner, was anxiously planning his film-watching itinerary.

Glenn *loves* movies.

I'm actually the planner for all our events, not just weddings, and I was already exhausted—I'd like to say that's why I'd been microwaving so many dinners lately, but who would I be kidding?—and the festival hadn't even begun. "That's why they call you the wedding *planner*," Mike pointed out when I complained to him.

"Oh, so I'm off the hook for event *implementation*? You going to take care of things when something goes wrong?"

"You're telling me I don't do that already?"

We were definitely tired: Mike and I don't snipe at each other quite like that normally. Well, maybe we do, though generally with less of an edge.

Still, along with the tiredness, a sense of anticipation and pre-accomplishment was gathering, too. It was all going to go well. We were hosting the Wedding of the Year, we had Big Names staying in our rooms and suites, and Adrienne the diva chef hadn't killed anybody.

Yet, I reminded myself. Early days. I went back to the interview and Brett started talking again. "I don't care who you are, life is a struggle. It's how you perceive those struggles. It's what you *do* with those struggles. That's what says who you are. But you know, I have to say, as I've gotten older, I take them more like just another day at the office. It's a matter of acceptance, isn't it? Acceptance of what the universe throws at you." He was managing to be both credit-claiming and Zen at the same time. Who said he couldn't act? "That's why I've made some decisions this year, and if they affect the way the public, the movie-going public, views me, then so be it."

A dramatic pause. "Here it comes," I told Ibsen.

Brett flashed his patented smile at the camera. "The first thing is, in case anyone cares, the truth is, I'm gay," he said.

"Big revelation," I said to Ibsen. Like no one could have figured that one out. Young, handsome, single, lives with another young handsome single guy. You tell me.

"And so here it is: this spring, I'm heading to Cape Cod for the premiere of my new movie, *Revenge,* at the fabulous Provincetown International Film Festival. And while I'm there, I'm getting married to my partner, Justin Braden."

"That's even his real name," I remarked to Ibsen. "Justin Braden. It sounds made-up, but it's real."

The interviewer had something to say for a minute, and then the camera swung back to Brett. "Provincetown is very open, very accepting," he said. "We thought it would be the best place to do it. The only place to do it, really. P'town makes it real. And it makes it personal. We didn't want a Hollywood sideshow."

And yet here you are, announcing it for the world to hear. I clicked off just as the phone rang, and I smiled when I looked at the caller ID. "Ali."

"Tell me you were just thinking of me," my boyfriend said.

"I'm always thinking of you," I said. "What did you have for dinner?"

"Garlic-butter steak, roasted potatoes, asparagus," he rattled off. Ali can cook. "You?"

I scowled at the rice and beans, now cooling off in a singularly unappetizing way. "Microwave. Prick and ping."

"Excuse me?"

"You prick the plastic, you put it in the microwave, it goes ping," I said.

5

He sighed. "Good thing I'm coming to rescue you from your culinary gulag."

"That's even if I have *time* for your cooking," I parried. "Seriously, it's faster to eat out."

"Even *you* can't get a table at a restaurant during the film festival, *cara*," he said. Ali is Lebanese-American, but he thinks Italian sounds sexy. Actually, he's right. "Karen has this gorgeous garlic shrimp-and-spinach recipe."

Karen is Ali's sister, and the Boston police commissioner, with less time on her hands on a normal day than we had on ours even during the worst of the festival. "Karen doesn't cook," I pointed out.

"I said she has the recipe. I didn't say she'd actually done anything with it."

"Uh-huh." I took a swallow of wine and settled back into the sofa, which obligingly did its Little Shop of Horrors routine around me. "When are you coming down?" Ali lives in Boston, three hours' drive—or a two-hour ferry ride, in the summer—north of Provincetown. I'd spent a month with him there in January, the inn's slowest time; he was scheduled to spend festival week with me.

"Monday," he said. No surprise there; the festival began on Wednesday, but the wedding was Tuesday evening, and Ali was a big Brett Falcone fan.

"Good," I said. "Ibsen misses you."

"No doubt. You need anything from the big city?"

I considered asking him to hit one of the warehouse liquor stores for wine, but stopped myself. Ali's Muslim and doesn't drink alcohol. He's not against it, or against me drinking it, it's just not part of who he is. Even so, the thought of him wandering around reading labels seemed a little much. "I'm good, thanks."

"Which means you have a freezer full of pizzas and a cupboard with four bottles of Côtes du Rhône."

"And a Chateâuneuf-du-Pape," I said defensively. "For a special occasion."

"I'll try to provide you with one."

"A bottle of wine?"

I could hear the sexy shift in his voice. "A special occasion, *cara*," Ali said.

I was still smiling when I went to bed.

***

"Brett and Justin," said Mike. "Christ, they couldn't sound more gay if they tried."

I gave him a look. "*You're* gay," I pointed out.

"Matching tuxes, too, right?"

"You know, anyone listening might think you were a homophobe," I said conversationally.

"I like to keep people guessing." Mike was leafing through the sheaf of requirements I'd deposited on his desk. "You got all this?"

"No doves," I said, shaking my head. "They wanted to release doves during the ceremony. We don't do doves."

"Thank God for that, anyway." He tossed the papers back on his desk and leveled a look at me. "You have any other weddings during the festival?" We generally have at least two or three a week for most of the summer; the Race Point Inn is Provincetown's most sought-after wedding venue. Partly thanks to Adrienne the diva chef, but partly, too, I like to think, because of me.

"Nope." I shook my head. "Someone else wanted to book Tuesday. I sent them over to Crowne Pointe."

He nodded and chewed his lower lip reflectively. "How many people for this one?"

"Small," I said. "By Hollywood stand-ards." I had no idea what that meant, but it sounded hip, and talking about things I know nothing about comes easily to me. That's how I roll. "Twenty-eight people, the grooms, their attendants." It was just about the maximum we could fit on the patio out beyond the swim-ming-pool where we had a bower and space for events. Anything over thirty-five, we had an agreement with the Pilgrim Monument for a tent on the lawn up at the top of High Pole Hill.

"Okay. You have a list?"

I must have looked startled. "A list? Of the guests?" That wasn't particularly standard. "They're all staying here, you should have their names."

"Only when they check in. They're all booked under Falcone." He wasn't looking at me. "So I looked, but you can't tell who is ac-tually coming, that's all."

I was staring at him. "Mike... what? what is it?"

He ran a hand over his head. Easier to do, these days, with a hairline that had receded by about a couple of miles since I'd first met him. Still a handsome man, for all of that, with clear blue eyes and an infectious smile. Which, of course, he wasn't manifesting just at the moment. "I think I know one of them," he mumbled. "One of the guests, I mean."

Not a happy thought, I diagnosed. "An old flame?" I asked, lightly, not thinking of what I was saying.

"An ex-husband," he said.

Cripes. The things you don't know about your co-workers. Irrationally, I found I was annoyed. One very cold October night, once upon a time during Fantasia Fair, Mike had saved my life. Fished me out of the harbor before I gave in to hypothermia. I'd thought that meant we were blood-siblings or something. To not know about a *marriage* in his past? What was he thinking? "You never told me," I said blankly.

"Never came up," he said. He was looking at a framed photograph on his desk. Two years ago, he'd fallen in love. Three months later we were standing together at a funeral. I'd ached more for Mike than I'd ever ached for my own losses; talk about being unlucky in love. "So who was he?" I asked.

"He was, and is, a producer," he said. "He did Brett Falcone's latest movie. The one they're showing at the festival. *Revenge.*" He paused. "Appropriate enough name."

That told me absolutely nothing. I have no idea what a producer does. I had no idea what any of that meant. But at the end of the day, it didn't really matter. The reality is, like it or not, fifty percent of marriages end in divorce, and why shouldn't gay marriages share in our heterosexual misery? And ex-spouses run into each other all the time; part of life here in the twenty-first century.

Still, Mike is my friend, and of course there was that whole saving my life business, and on top of that, he looked miserable. "You could take the day off?" I suggested hopefully.

He gave me a look. Mike is nothing if not a micromanager. Benign, yes, but a micromanager all the same. On the other hand... enough was enough: you can't mourn forever, or hang on to a slight forever, and I had no idea how I was supposed to respond to his revelation. "What do you want me to say?" I asked. "He was an idiot to let you go? He has a lot of nerve coming to stay at your inn? He should go on a whale watch and jump over the side?" *Well, okay, stop, Riley, the latter might be too tempting.* I paused. "It sucks, Mike. I'm sorry. For the record, if I'd been married to you, I'd never have let you go."

"Oh, please. Like I'd ever marry a *girl*."

Oh, good: there was the Mike I knew and loved. "There you go. And, besides, look on the bright side. With all those guests, there are bound to be some unattached handsome actors or directors or something. Maybe you'll score."

"For a straight girl, you have a dirty mind," he informed me.

"It's why you love me so," I agreed and blew him a kiss. I hesitated at the door, guilt catching me up. "Hey, Mike—you're all right? I mean, really?"

"I'm all right," he agreed.

I wasn't at all sure I believed him. But I also didn't really have time to figure it out. Later, of course, I'd wish I had. But who knows what evil lurks in the heart of man?

The shadow knows, I could hear Ali's voice in my head. He's a fan of the old Shadow series, too.

I acknowledged the new kid at the reception desk—Mike and Glenn seem to have a never-ending supply of young fiercely attractive young men to work there, and the summer contingent had arrived for the season—and sat down at the desk in what I euphemistically call my office. It's a former closet, actually; Barry, my first boss at the inn, had taken off the door and all the insides, made the framework into an elegant archway, stuck a desk and chair there and called it a day. Receptionists were constantly bumping into me, but square footage is just as valuable in P'town as it is in New York City, and I counted my blessings. I had a big calendar up on the wall and a Mac Mini on the desk and that was it.

Just the one wedding this week, but a VIP party to organize on Wednesday night—the after-party for the opening celebration down at the Crown & Anchor—and a reception on Thursday, a VIP breakfast on Friday, two private parties on Saturday, and by Sunday, the last day of the festival, we all collapse. I wasn't actually in charge of the nuts-and-bolts of all these events, but I was definitely in charge of seeing they all happened smoothly.

Now there's a happy thought.

2

On Sunday, Mirela called just as I was starting to think about dinner, and wondering whether I could afford to eat it at the inn's main restaurant. They give me a discount, but, hell, it's still Provincetown prices. "Hello, sunshine, and what is happening?" Mirela is Bulgarian, and she thinks sunshine is an endearment. She's not very good with irony or sarcasm. Nor, for that matter, with contractions.

"I'm hungry," I said. "That's about all."

She laughed, her voice running up and down the scale. Mirela's laugh has people stopping in the street to see where that beautiful sound is coming from... and then once they see her, they keep staring because she is, to coin a cliché, drop-dead gorgeous. "Then eat," she said.

"Just consulting my financial advisor before I invest," I said. She wouldn't understand. Mirela came to P'town with absolutely nothing but her work ethic, part of the wave of Bulgarian students who arrive here every summer, young and strong and wanting to be somebody. They take on three or four jobs and fit eight people into a one-bedroom rental and generally keep the town running before heading back home in the fall.

Mirela had stayed on, once she'd discovered she could develop what she thought of as a modest interest in painting—Provincetown is America's oldest continuously operating art colony—into a full-blown career. She bought a condo in the West End, shows her work at a prestigious gallery, and makes more money selling one painting than I do in three or four months working at the inn.

"Oh, sunshine," she said impatiently. "Never mind the money. I will take you to dinner."

I didn't waste any time. Offer me a free dinner in P'town in the summer? I'm there. "Okay," I said. "I *can* be bought. Meet you at the inn in an hour. I won't be able to get us a table, but we can sit at the bar." A thought occurred. "Why did you call, anyway?"

The laugh again. "I'll tell you in an hour," she said, mischief in her voice, and disconnected.

I didn't have time to think about it, because the phone rang again and it was the great man, Brett Falcone himself. "Just wanted to make sure you don't need anything else from me," he said. "We're flying out tonight. Probably get to P'town on the afternoon ferry tomorrow."

"Excellent," I said. "Everything's fine here." I'd have said the same thing even if it wasn't. Being a wedding organizer is all about being calm and reassuring, no matter what might be blowing up around you. I trotted out my usual line. "Are you excited?"

"About getting married?"

No; about taking the red-eye to Boston. "Of course," I said cheerfully.

"Yeah, we are. Justin's nervous. I guess I'm not, because I'm used to, you know, getting up in front of people. He's always behind the scenes, so he's afraid he's going to trip coming down the aisle or something, you know?"

I nodded, then remembered he couldn't see me. "I'm sure he'll be fine," I said. Justin Braden was a screenwriter; it was how they'd met, five or six years ago. I had yet to see anyone trip during a wedding, but there's a first time for everything. "Tell him hello from me, and I'll see you both tomorrow."

With Ali coming, possibly on the same ferry, it was going to be a crowded day.

Mirela was waiting for me in the bar, flirting with the bartender. She flirts a lot with gay men; she says it helps her keep in practice. "Sunshine! I have ordered you a cocktail."

I slid onto the stool next to her and looked up as the bartender pushed a napkin across to me, followed by something colorful with fruit and mint on top. "Thanks, Ken," I said. *What the hell is this?* "What am I drinking, anyway?"

"Fleur de Guadalupe," he said carelessly. I was none the wiser, but prudently didn't pursue it and took a cautious sip. Rum. Oh, boy. A lot of rum.

"It is the Moroccan bitters," Mirela assured me. "They make the difference."

Ken said, quietly, "it's the ginger beer."

She glared at him. Mirela hates being contradicted. "Never mind," she said. "It is good. And we will want a menu."

I ignored them and took another sip of Ken's concoction. "So what's up?" I asked Mirela.

She gave an exaggerated sigh. "You are always so quick, Americans," she said. "Enjoy yourself first. Drink. Relax for a few minutes. When is Ali coming?"

Despite having practically nothing that I can see in common between them, Ali and Mirela are amazingly close friends. Like, close friends *forever*. Then again, it's possible they have more in common than I have with him. Who knows what the secret sauce of relationships is? "Tomorrow," I said.

"*That* is why you do not want to cook tonight," she declared. "You want to keep your apartment clean."

Like my apartment is ever clean. Nice one. I finally lost patience. "What is *up*, Mirela?" A thought occurred. "Is it about Guy?"

Guy Husband, underwater treasure-hunter and Rich Dude. He'd swept into Provincetown in November to raise the Mignon-ette, part of the pirate fleet of Black Sam Bellamy that went down in a storm in 1717. He'd raised more than any of us had bargained for… and captured Mirela's heart in the meantime. But he was back in England now; she hadn't mentioned him for months, and had resisted my numerous attempts to find out what was going on.

She twirled her drink in the glass. Ken brought us menus. We both ignored them. "It is not Guy," she said. "All right. I will tell you. But you must promise not to become upset."

"There is no way to *not* be upset after someone says that," I pointed out. Am I right? "Come on, Mirela."

She wasn't looking at me. "I am going to go home next week."

Whatever I might have been expecting, it wasn't that. "Home? In the *summer*?" Summer is a Provincetown artist's most lucrative time. It's when the rest of the world somehow realizes that we've got some of the most amazing artists in the world here: Cynthia Packard, John Dowd, Ed Walsh, TJ Walton, Marian Roth. The world ignores us all winter long and suddenly "finds" us in the season.

Not that Mirela was ever short of money, but still, I'd never known her to go anywhere in the summer. Not even "over the bridge," as we refer to going off-Cape. "What happened? *Did* something happen?" Mirela doesn't often talk about her family, or—now that I thought about it—much about her past at all. I knew she came from a city called Plovdiv, alternately called Bulgaria's "cultural capital" and its "hidden gem" (hey, I can Google with the best of them), and that her father was someone important in the financial sector there. I'd seen an old photograph of her in the Bulgarian national folk costume—which I will *never* allow her to live down—and another of her onstage at some theatre festival. For someone who was allegedly my best friend, there was a paucity of information there.

"It is," she said, and paused, "a delicate subject."

"Okay. I can be delicate."

"It is my sister," she said. I didn't know she had a sister. "She is about to have a baby." She sighed and took a sip of her cocktail. "It is complicated. The baby's father is married— and much older. He is a colleague of our father."

I raised my eyebrows. "I can see where that would complicate things."

"She is also engaged to be married," added Mirela. "To someone else, another man. The marriage is… important. It is not a good situation." There was a pause.

"So you're going over to help her out? To be the baby's godmother or something?" I had no idea where she was going with this.

"No," said Mirela. "I think what it is, I think they expect me to adopt this baby and bring it here."

***

I probably should have listened more closely to Mirela. I was going to regret not following up with her—or following up with Mike, either, for that matter. I'm getting good at ignoring clues when they're strewn directly in my path, but I had no idea how to respond to her, and I had other things on my mind.

That's my story, anyway, and I'm sticking to it.

Ali was on the second afternoon ferry, as it turned out, and I barely made it to the dock at MacMillan Pier on time to meet him; there was some problem in the kitchen and Adrienne the diva chef had gone into a tailspin. You could probably hear the screaming in Vermont. Not an auspicious beginning to film-festival week.

I stood shielding my eyes from the sun and scrutinized the passengers, the sound of wheeled suitcases clattering all around me and gulls screaming overhead, demanding their due in dropped sandwiches and fried onion rings from John's Footlong.

Snippets of conversation floated by.

"I told him we'd meet up at Tea Dance…"

"He called too late for a reservation, but I said, honey, I am *not* spending a week in a *campground* this summer…"

"Isn't that Joshua? Hey, Josh!"

And then Ali was there and I had the over-all physical response I still get every time I see him after an absence, a sort of thrill that starts at my toes and goes up to my head, flushing my cheeks an unbecoming red and, for some obscure reason, making me tongue-tied. "Ali!"

"*Cara.*" We were off to a great start if he was already using his Italian endearments.

Ali is seriously the most beautiful human being on the planet. He has olive-toned skin thanks to his Lebanese DNA, with black hair that flops a little over his forehead, permanent designer stubble on his chin, and eyes you can get lost in. I lost no time getting lost in them.

There wasn't much of an opportunity for it, though, because almost immediately over his shoulder I caught sight of Gretchen Callender. "We need to go," I said urgently, reaching over to grab his carryall. "I'll take this."

"What's the rush?"

Gretchen Callender was the executive director of the Provincetown International Film Society and, therefore, of the film festival. There was only one reason she could be meeting the ferry in person. Or, rather, two reasons: Brett Falcone and Justin Braden. I didn't want to be part of that welcoming party; I was going to have more than enough star exposure the next day. This moment was just for me and Ali.

He'd followed my gaze, though, just in time to see them—complete with entourage—engulf Gretchen. "Isn't that him? Brett Falcone?"

I sighed. "Yes. We can grab a taxi if—"

"I'm a fan, you know."

I slanted him a look. "I know."

"And—"

"And you'll have plenty of time to chat with him," I said firmly, turning us both around and heading back up the pier. It was crowded enough to make it an exercise in frustration—hell, trying to get anywhere in the summertime in Provincetown is an exercise in frustration—but the pier when a ferry's just come in is spectacularly crowded. Once upon a time, the railroad tracks came all the way down to the end of the wharf, picked people up from the ferries. And they didn't even have wheelie suitcases then.

We made it to my apartment without losing quite half our body weights in sweat, and I got the lemonade out. "So," I said.

"So," Ali echoed. He was fighting the tendency of both my couch and my cat to try and smother him.

"Dinner tonight," I said. "You get to meet your idol."

"He's not my idol," he protested. "Just a really great actor."

"Uh-huh." I handed him his glass and then perched on the other chair in the room. People who think New York City apartments are small haven't visited non-second-home owners' places in P'town. "Mike's in a tizzy. It turns out, you won't believe this, he used to be married to Brett's producer. Well, the producer for this movie. I can't remember what it's called."

"*Revenge*," said Ali. Ibsen was trying to lick his hair.

"*Revenge*, then. Fitting title, huh? He didn't say, but it was clear that it still hurt—I think Mike really fell for this guy."

"The fact of a marriage," he said, "kind of gives that away."

I raised my eyebrows. Ali and I met when he was an ICE investigator trying to see if any of the inn's weddings were fraudulent. They weren't, but he *had* to have had some cynicism about the institution to have been doing that kind of investigating in the first place.

The phone spared me from answering. I looked at the screen. "It's Brett," I told Ali. "Be good."

"Who, me?" He managed to look hurt. I swiped the phone. "Hey, Brett."

"Sydney! We got here!" There was a lot of noise in the background.

"So I gather," I said carefully. "Welcome to Provincetown."

"Come join us for a drink," he said. "I can't believe we're getting married tomorrow! This is fantastic! We can't wait to meet you in person! We're already having such a great time!"

"I'm very happy for you," I said. "Are you at the Race Point? My boyfriend and I will be over there later—"

"No, no, we're at Ross' Grill!" He had to shout over the noise; it made everything seem like an exclamation. "Checking out Whaler's

Wharf! You simply *have* to come over here and join us!"

I sighed. Whaler's Wharf was one place in town I really *didn't* want to be. The Province-town International Film Society's main office is there, along with miscellaneous spaces and two modest-sized projection rooms rather grandly referred to as Water's Edge Cinema. On the eve of the film festival, it was going to be mobbed.

Not that it isn't in June, anyway.

The whole complex started out as a real wharf, back when Provincetown was a major whaling port and the ships came here to un-load their cargoes of blubber and other un-mentionable parts of the whales they finally hunted nearly to extinction. Sometime in the mid-1800s, Yankee schooners were sailing to rich whaling grounds off the Azores islands and returning with skilled Portuguese seamen. Those seamen settled here, and it turned Prov-incetown into a Portuguese fishing village.

Later, much later, when the ships no longer came and most of the piers had been destroyed by winter storms, the wharf build-ing was converted into the Provincetown The-ater (for movies, not plays, unlike the *current* Provincetown Theater up on Bradford Street), and the broken-up pieces of stone announcing it as such—which once formed an impressive proscenium arch over the entryway—were now behind the building on the beach. These days the Wharf doesn't extend over the water anymore, but instead its three floors are filled with small offices and smart shops and artisans offering everything from Tarot card readings to homemade fudge, with Ross' Grill on the second floor at the back offering a spectacular view of the harbor. The food is frankly amazing and the wine list impressive and both of them are way out of my affordability range.

And, like I said, everyone and their Aunt Edna was bound to be there right now.

Still, this was why they paid me the medium bucks, so I made a face at Ali and took a deep breath. "Okay, Brett, we'll meet you there in—what? An hour? Does that work?"

"Sure! We're staying here for dinner, why don't you plan on joining us? We'd love to have you. You know, get to know you a little. We'll hold a couple of seats for you!" He sounded like he'd already been hitting the champagne pretty hard.

Dinner at Ross' and not at the inn, as I'd so carefully arranged? That was bound to go over well with Adrienne the diva chef. And

Mike. And Martin the maître d'. Not, I reminded myself, my problem. "See you there," I said to Brett, and disconnected. I looked at Ali. "They're at Ross' Grill," I said. "We're to join them for dinner."

"Great!" He approved of the restaurant. Ali still works for ICE, and Ross' wasn't normally in *his* budget, either. "I'll have the duck."

"You have the menu memorized?" I demanded, staring at him.

"Always need to know what to order, just in case I ever found myself there. And, see, I was right!"

"There you go. Simple aspirations." I didn't like the fact that Brett was going off-script (dinner had been planned for them at the inn, after all, and if he was already doing things that weren't in the plan it didn't bode well for the rest of the week, which was pretty tightly scheduled—but again, once we got beyond the wedding itself, not my problem), but there wasn't much I could do about it, and if this was as far off as he was going to get, it wasn't too egregious in the greater scheme of things.

Boy, can I ever be wrong.

3

Ali was inclined to take his time; this was, after all, a vacation for him. I was less so: I wanted to get the whole thing over with and get back home and into bed. I was not without an agenda; we had, after all, a little catching-up to do in that department.

And the star-studded wedding was tomorrow.

We managed to make it to Whaler's Wharf without poking our heads into more than two or three galleries on the way. The building was, as I'd expected, jammed with people. Already you could see the ubiquitous lanyards and nametags the film festival gave out, identifying passholders, press, and VIPs, hanging proudly around people's necks. Or, rather, the people wearing seemed to be proud of the lanyards.

As perhaps they should—the top-level pass costs well over a thousand dollars. If I spent that kind of money, I'd want something to show for it, too.

We walked along the ground floor, which was almost like walking along a quaint street, as the building's open to the sky in the center. It was pleasant, really, and I told myself to relax. I wasn't the one dealing with Adrienne the diva chef. I wasn't the one dealing with anything, tonight, but a nice dinner and then quality time with my boyfriend. We took the stairway that circled the rotunda to get to the restaurant.

I was right about Brett; he was definitely enjoying the bubbles. "Sydney!" He grabbed me and did air-kisses on either cheek. It was a little awkward, as we'd never actually met in person, but Brett was a professional schmoozer, and hey, I do weddings for a living. We went through the "my partner, Justin," and "my partner, Ali" thing, and then Justin—every bit as good-looking as Brett—was talking about organizing drinks for us.

Ali requested a ginger ale, and Justin frowned. "We have some really nice Dom Perignon," he said. "You sure you won't have any?" I'd already grabbed a flute as the waiter—clearly there to take care of the party—hovered delicately. I wondered when exactly this had been arranged; it clearly wasn't something they'd just thought of. "No, really, just ginger ale, thanks," said Ali.

Comprehension dawned on the groom-to-be. "Oh, of course, sorry," he said. "You're in a program. Sorry. Seems like everybody is, these days. Half of Hollywood, anyway. In a program, in rehab, in something."

"Actually," said Ali mildly, "I'm just Muslim."

Justin stared at him, reassessing. Maybe wondering how he could fit it into a script somewhere. "Cool," he finally said, and turned to the waiter. "Can you get a ginger ale?" he asked.

Brett called across the table at the group, slowly starting to find places at the table for dinner. "Everyone, this is Sydney! She's in charge of the wedding!" A small cheer went dutifully up.

I sipped my champagne and surveyed the room. Ours wasn't the only party there, but it was still early enough that the real crowd hadn't begun to gather. In fact, the *sunset* hadn't even begun yet; the sky over the harbor was clear and blue and nearly cloudless.

Ali got his drink and Brett seemed to notice us again. "You don't mind we're here, Sydney? Justin used to come here when he summered in P'town. And we straightened it out with Mike and Matthew—is that his name?"

"Martin? The maître d'?"

"That's the one," he said. "Paid for dinner there, we insisted. Just wanted to make my boy happy, you know?"

"Whatever works for the two of you," I said. "This is your wedding." I'd been saying that a lot to them, all through the planning. The words were getting to be very automatic. This is your day. This is your event. This is your wedding.

Brett turned to Ali. "I hope you'll come?" he asked, flashing his patented Crest-white smile. "To the ceremony? and the reception? As our guest?"

Ali glanced at me, his expression clearly telegraphing *why not?* "I'd be glad to," he said.

"Good, then." The smile really *was* as dazzling in person as it was at the movies. "Glad to meet you." He made a circular swirling gesture with his hand. "Gotta circulate."

"What the hell was that?" I asked Ali as soon as Brett moved away. We stood shoulder to shoulder watching him go.

"An invitation," Ali said.

"Looked more like a tornado to me," I said.

Dinner was duly ordered and served, but as I'd had enough to drink that I needed the toilets, I excused myself from the table. I wasn't the only one with that in mind; there was a line for the bathroom, and I'd left it a little late.

But… no worries. Whaler's Wharf has secret restrooms reserved for occupants of the offices and for the rent-paying artisans to use. I'm not supposed to have the key… but I have the key. And I actually was carrying my keys, for once, a minor miracle in itself. I headed over to the other side of the building, past the fountain sparking in the rotunda, and up into the narrow cubby off a landing in the front stairwell as quickly and smoothly as I could, thanking my lucky stars I had the option. I really, really needed to go. Everything was, all in all, off to a good start. We'd finish a fabulous expensive dinner, watch the sunset reflecting in the clouds over the harbor, and still catch an early night.

The duck Ali had ordered at Ross' might not have been a lucky one, I was thinking, but I sure was.

Right until the moment I unlocked the toilet and saw the body on the floor, that is.

***

Everyone came. The police—well, fair play, I'd been the one who made the call, so I couldn't complain about their arrival, though to be honest it took them longer than I liked. Everyone else? Why are we all so fascinated with other people's tragedies? Schadenfreude must be the most despicable of all human emotions.

And did they ever come! People emptying out of the cinema. Festival-goers with their lanyards, tourists hoping for a bit of drama, the whole of whoever happened to be working at Whaler's Wharf and their Aunt Edna.

I'd closed the bathroom door behind me with the body inside, made sure it was locked, and stood resolutely in front of it waiting for the police. *Breathe, Riley, breathe*, I counseled myself. And called Ali. "I'm not coming back," I said.

"Where are you?"

"Down the hall," I said. "Other end of the building. Um… there's a dead woman here."

There was a moment of silence. "You didn't just say a dead woman."

"I did," I said miserably.

Another silence. Duck dinner or no, my boyfriend was not a happy camper. I should mention, perhaps, that this wasn't the first dead body I'd ever seen. My friend Julie, who heads up Provincetown's detective squad, claims I go looking for them, but that's simply not true. They find me. No, really. They do.

He sighed, loudly enough that I could hear it over the phone. "Where *are* you?" he asked again, and this time there was exasperation in his voice.

"Look," I said. "I don't even *know* her, okay?" Which made something of a change from some of the other dead people I've run across, people I knew, in some cases people I cared deeply about. Where they hell were the police? I had no business protecting a crime scene. Hell, I had no business being within ten miles of a crime scene. "Don't come, it's ridiculously crowded here already."

"I can't come," he said reasonably. "You still haven't told me where you are."

"Oh. Right. I'm at one of the staff bath-rooms."

"Ross' Grill staff?"

"No, they don't have their own bathroom. For Whaler's Wharf. Up in the front, toward Commercial Street. They keep it locked so the tourists don't use it."

"And you just happen to have the key?"

Well, yes. That was going to take some ex-plaining. I hoped Mirela's artist friend Régine didn't get thrown out because of that key. "I borrowed it once," I said, a little defensively.

"And forgot to return it. *Seriously*, Riley?"

Uh-oh. Not only was this not the way I'd planned to spend the evening, it looked like my romantic night was in peril, too. Ali only uses my last name when he's completely exas-perated. We were a long way from this after-noon's Italian endearments.

"I'll call you back," I said, and discon-nected.

A body in a locked room. Professor Plum in the library. Why did my life sometimes feel like I was playing a bit part in a perfect murder mystery?

Julie, when she arrived, was clearly and in big capital letters Not Amused. "I might have known," she said darkly. "What do you have, a special dead-body radar? Some homicide alarm goes off in your head?"

At least she wasn't immediately assuming I was a suspect; that was something. Progress. "I had to use the bathroom," I said, a little defensively. I still did, actually.

"Of course you did," she said. "Don't go away." My key—well, the key I used—was still in the door; she snapped on a pair of gloves, turned the knob, slipped into the bathroom. The bathroom is in a sort of anteroom between floors; her uniformed underlings were taping the stairway off, moving onlookers back.

I wondered if Julie would shoot me if I left. Probably.

She came out again, a woman's change purse in her hand. "You know someone named Caroline Cooper?"

I shook my head.

"Well, that's something, anyway," said Julie, still reading the driver's license. She gestured to one of the officers in the stairwell. "Check out the cinema," she said. "This woman's from Los Angeles, she's got to be with one of the film groups."

I swallowed. "Um—Julie—"

She didn't even look up from sifting through the cards in the purse. "No."

"Julie."

"Tell me you're not going to tell me something I don't want to hear."

"They're in the restaurant," I said. "The film people."

The change purse closed with a snap. "And you know this *how?* No, wait. Let me guess. You were having dinner with her."

"Well, yes… but I didn't kill her," I said. "I didn't even *meet* her." When she was alive, anyway. "Ali's still there." I took a deep breath. "And I still need the toilet."

"Not this one, you don't. Bill! Check Ross' Grill. Apparently that's where she came from." She looked at me. "You can go back, there, too, but don't talk about this. We'll do the talking. I want to get as much information as I can before the boys from South Yarmouth get here."

"You're saying this is murder," I said. In Massachusetts, homicides are the purview of the state police. The barracks in South Yarmouth investigated on behalf of the Cape & Islands district attorney's office.

"All I'm saying is she's deceased," said Julie. But she wouldn't call the Staties in if she thought it was a heart attack. "Now, get."

I stopped at the public toilets on my way back to the restaurant. The group's merriment had died down; a cop at the door was keeping everyone inside, and there was an air of unease hanging over the tables over which Brett and Justin presided. I slipped back into the seat next to Ali.

He took my hand. "You okay?"

I nodded. Julie was coming into the room, having a word with the host. A moment later the music was turned off. Her eyes traveled over our tables. "Excuse me. I'm sorry to interrupt your dinner. I'm with the Provincetown police. Does anyone here know Caroline Cooper?"

That got immediate reactions from our crowd; they all did. There was an empty chair two seats down from Justin; I knew Julie had clocked it already. The woman across from me looked sick; a second later she slid off her seat and onto the floor. No one moved to help her.

Brett was on his feet. "Where's Caroline? What's happened?"

Julie came over to the table. "And you are?" she asked. I wondered if she really didn't recognize him or if this was just standard cop-talk.

He looked at her in amazement. It couldn't have been a reaction he got every day. "Brett Falcone," he said.

"Please sit down, Mr. Falcone." Another cop came in and spoke in her ear for a moment. She nodded and turned back to the table as he left. "Was Ms. Cooper here with you?"

Brett sat down. Slowly, as though to make a point. "Right there," he said, gesturing at the empty chair. There was a salad on the plate in front of it, forlorn and untouched.

"Did anyone notice her leave?"

"Are you going to tell us what happened?" He sounded truculent; he hadn't liked being told what to do, though film directors must have done it to him every day.

She gave him the same look she'd been giving me since she'd arrived. Like he was a dubious fashion she wasn't sure would catch on. "I'm sorry to tell you that Caroline Cooper is deceased."

Another stir; gasps around the table, exclamations. Someone finally got up and went over to the woman who'd fainted. "Hell of a time to revive her," I muttered to Ali. "She'll faint all over again when she hears that."

He squeezed my hand. "Be good."

"What happened?" It was Justin, looking. Little pale around the gills himself.

Julie ignored him. "We'll need everyone's name and contact information, and then you're free to go," she said. It was more than a hint, even though no one was in the mood to continue with the party; Julie was showing who was in charge.

For now, anyway.

4

The show was, apparently, to go on.

All of them, in fact. The film society wasted no time in putting a sad little note up on its website announcing Caroline Cooper's untimely demise, expressing condolences to her friends and family, and making it clear that the schedule wasn't being changed: movies, parties, workshops and events would all proceed as planned.

And Brett and Justin made it equally clear that the wedding was still on. "Well," Brett said to me on the telephone, "it wasn't as if she was even here *just* for the wedding, you know, even though of course we invited her. And she was in the wedding party. But not primarily." He was talking a lot; I wondered why. "She was here for revenge."

"What?" I was sure I hadn't heard him right. Revenge on whom?

"*Revenge*," he said, impatience creeping into his voice. "Our movie."

Oh, right. "What did she do?" I asked. "I mean, with regards to the movie?"

"Co-producer," he said. "With Austin Hyde." His voice was meaningful; I was supposed to recognize the famous name. I didn't, but I knew exactly who he was anyway: Mike's ex-husband. This was developing into a regular Peyton Place of interconnected stories.

"So we're leaving everything in place?" I asked. Ali, sitting on the sofa and stroking Ibsen, looked up, his eyebrows raised. I shrugged at him.

"This," said Brett, "is the most important thing I'll ever do." It sounded like a line from a film; I wondered what *Revenge* was about. Besides the title, of course. "Justin and I talked it over, and we're in agreement. I'm sorry about Caroline, of course I am, but the wedding's going forward. We're not letting anything stand in the way."

"Okay," I said. "See you tomorrow, then." The film festival had hardly begun and already I'd had enough of Hollywood.

Not that this was any of my business. As I'd told Julie, I hadn't even known the dead woman.

***

The next day I found out just how insane these people were.

The inn had filled up, every room booked, the restaurant wasn't taking reservations, and Glenn looked like he was going to have a heart attack. I sat with him at the breakfast table and watched the display, the same thing you see at all the parties, people coming into the room with big smiles plastered on their faces, looking around to see what important person might be there. They'd smile brightly at you, ready to become enthusiastic should you be someone they wanted to impress, then slide their eyes away to look past you if you weren't a VIP. Still with that same bright smile. "Someone threatened to ruin me if they couldn't get a room for Saturday," Glenn said gloomily.

"A good problem to have," I said, sipping coffee.

"What, me getting ruined? That's a good problem? Heaven help me if I ever have a bad one, then. And on top of that, there's the festival. I've got all my films picked out and I can't find my tickets."

"I'm sure they'll issue you new ones," I said, as comfortingly as I could. Tickets were reserved and paid for online, but one had to go to a temporary box office for them to be printed out. Some people got theirs early; it didn't surprise me Glenn was one of them. He was, in his own way, a VIP.

"And that thing at Whaler's Wharf... You were there, weren't you?"

"I was," I said a little wearily. "And Glenn, before you say anything, I didn't have anything to do with them switching dinner plans."

He waved that away. "It's okay. They squared it with Mike, and we had three dinner services. It all worked out. Besides, maybe it's just as well. If she'd been here, she'd have gotten herself killed here. What we don't need is another body."

There was a short silence. Years ago, the Race Point Inn had been the scene of another murder—Barry, my boss and Glenn's partner. I'd been the one to find him floating in the pool. It was something neither of us was ever going to forget. I sighed. "Maybe you're right.

I'll have to mend some bridges with Martin and Adrienne, though, I suspect."

"They'll survive," said Glenn. He was going back to being morose. "I hate sending overflow to Crowne Pointe," he said.

"You hate sending overflow anywhere," I reminded him. "And listen to me: it's a good problem to have."

The room was filling up, and a couple had just come in. They glanced around and wandered over to our four-top. "Do you mind if we join you? Seems pretty busy," the man said. Forties, I thought, with a slick moustache. The woman was blonde and slightly younger. They both wore the film festival's ubiquitous lanyard.

Glenn gestured. "Of course," he said, looking not at them but at me. I mouthed "good problem" at him and nodded encouragingly.

"Great, thanks." The man didn't hold the chair for the woman and she didn't seem to expect him to. Colleagues, I surmised, rather than a couple.

"I'm Sydney," I said. We're in the hospitality business, might as well act hospitable. "And this is Glenn."

"Jack Donnelly," the man said heartily. "Hi, Cindy, good to meet you." The blonde was fiddling with her phone and seemed to notice the prolonged pause after he spoke. I was wondering whether it was worth correcting him about my name. Naw. "Oh," she said, looking up at us blankly. "Sorry. I'm Irene. Irene Sandler."

"Film buffs?" I asked politely.

"God no," she said and laughed. "We're press."

"Speak for yourself," said Jack. "I'm the biggest film buff here."

She shook her head. "You can't just watch. It's hard work. You get to watch them, but then you have to write about them all. It's hard work."

He smiled at me. "Small price to pay."

A waiter came bustling up, looking horrified. "Sorry," he said to Glenn. "I didn't realize you had guests."

Glenn did the magnanimous-gesture thing again. "It's all good," he said. He clearly didn't know quite what was expected of him here.

Jack and Irene both ordered Bloody Marys to start, and the waiter left. "So what was that about?" Jack gestured at the waiter's retreating back. He seemed to do a lot of smiling.

50

"He was trying to impress the boss," I said. "Glenn owns the Race Point Inn."

"Oh, gosh!" He, at any rate, seemed genuinely impressed. "Wow. I mean, you do a great job! We love it here. This is the best inn in town!"

"Thank you," said Glenn. He stood up. "I don't mean to be rude, but…"

"Of course," said Jack, bending himself into that half-standing thing men do to indicate they're being polite. "You must have tons to do. Nice to meet you, Glenn."

I drank some more coffee and cast around for something to say. I finally came up with the dullest of all possible conversations. "Who do you write for?"

Irene said, "I'm with the *Hollywood Reporter*," she said. She put up an elegant hand. "And I know, I know, before you say it, I know what you're going to say, we don't usually do reviews." I actually wasn't going to say anything of the sort. "But we're covering the major festivals this year, just to add a little *je ne sais quoi*. Step out of our rut."

I had no idea how to respond. I'm not a Hollywood insider. "And how about you?" I asked Jack instead.

"I used to write for *Movieline*," he said.

51

Irene was nodding. "And we *all* know what happened with *Movieline*," she said, inspecting her fingernails. They were perfect. "Poor Jack."

"I used to be one of their top reviewers," he told me.

"Of course, that was twenty years ago," put in Irene. There was a gleam in her eye that said maybe she and Jack weren't as close buddies as they seemed.

Jack ignored her. "I was away for a while, but now I'm back, *and* writing for *Entertainment*," he said. A dig back at her. These were very pleasant people, really they were. "Do you know a lot about film reviews, Cindy?"

"Sydney," I said, automatically. "I occasionally *go* to the movies," I offered. "But that's about it."

Jack laughed, the little moment of pique gone. "That's all right. We like to think we're important in our little world, but there's no reason anyone else should think so," he said.

The waiter brought their drinks and I seized the moment to stand up in my turn. "I have to go, too," I said. "Nice to have met you. I hope you enjoy the festival."

Jack did his polite thing again and I went to my office. My chair was occupied by a woman who was crying—loudly—and the front desk staffed by a terrified-looking kid. Bernard? Bertrand? Something like that. "What's going on?"

He looked back at her helplessly. "She just came and asked for tissues," he said. "And when I turned my back to get some, she came behind the desk—just like that—and said never mind, she'd get them herself. So I told her she wasn't allowed behind the desk, and she just grabbed your chair and sat down and started crying, and I can't move her!"

"Do we know who she is? What room she's in?" I prepared myself to cope. The week was young, and I already had one murder and a hysterical crying woman on my hands.

He shook his head. "These people are *crazy*," he whispered.

"Tell me about it."

***

I'd probably had a few more hectic wedding days, but I couldn't bring them to mind right away. Or at all.

Ali had reached Mirela and was texting me all morning. *Why didn't you tell me she's going to Bulgaria?*

For heaven's sake. *Because we haven't had time,* I texted back.

I can't believe you didn't say anything. Aren't you upset?

If I took time to think about it, I reflected, I probably would be. *There's this dead person that got in the way.*

He wasn't amused. *I'm having lunch with her. See you at the wedding.*

I thought of all the things I could text back, and jammed the phone into my pocket instead. Everyone had issues today, it seemed. Glenn was worried about what to do with guest overflow and how to get to his precious movie viewing while running an inn. Mike was, last I saw, trying to do his job while stealthily checking out every room he went into, presumably in case his ex was lurking in one of them. I caught him in the afternoon being surreptitious in the empty breakfast room. "Are you looking for someone?"

He jumped. "Sydney!" He paused as if gathering his thoughts. "No, no, just making sure everything's okay."

No one had been in the room since brunch was over. "Are *you* okay?"

"Fine. Fine. Why wouldn't I be fine?"

I cast back to the name I'd heard. "Austin Hyde," I said.

He flinched. Visibly. "Good God, Sydney."

I wanted to touch his arm or his shoulder, show solidarity, but he looked like it might just send him off the deep end. I took a breath. "You're going to have to see him eventually," I reminded him. The wedding was in two hours. "You know that."

He suddenly looked about fifteen years old, and my heart went out to him. "Sit down," I said, taking a chair off the nearest table and seating myself in it, gesturing toward another. I was a little surprised when he took it down and lowered himself into it, gingerly, the way you do with bathwater that's just a little too hot. "Tell me about him," I said.

"We got married the day Massachusetts made marriage equality into law," he said. "We were lined up at the clerk's office."

"In P'town?"

He shook his head. "Cambridge. Austin had been sick all that year—pneumonia, he was hospitalized twice—and I couldn't get to him" His gaze left me and traveled around the empty room. Looking at the far wall as though transfixed, he told the rest of the story. "I

spent hours in all these hospital hallways, leaning against the wall, shredding Styrofoam coffee cups, waiting, because his father wouldn't
let me see him. Said he'd get a restraining order. We'd had a civil union done in Vermont,
but he wouldn't've let that stand in the way.
Austin's dad has the ear of the governor, the
senator, everyone who's anyone. He wasn't
bluffing. So it wasn't that I couldn't make decisions for him, I couldn't even *see* him." His
eyes were on the table but the past was open
in front of him. "He got better, and it was all
okay, but what about the next time? What
about when it was me?" He shrugged; the
questions were rhetorical.

"Scary times," I said when another pause
stretched out and I started wondering if there
were a chance for the conversation to continue.

Mike nodded. "Scary times," he agreed.
"You weren't doing weddings back then?"

"2004? Have a heart, that's a little before
my time."

"I didn't think so." He sighed, shifted position in his chair, finally brought his eyes to
mine. "It was magical that day, Sydney, you
have no idea. As if the confetti never ended.
Austin and me—we'd been together twelve

years by then. We didn't go to clubs. We didn't do Internet chat rooms. We cooked dinners together and went to Red Sox games and worried about the mortgage. Just like you." Well, maybe if I *had* a mortgage, I'd worry about it. Just getting by with the rent was good enough for me.

Mike still retains the slightest Louisiana accent, an echo of his home in the land of *laissez les bon temps rouler*, where it would be unimaginable to deliberately keep enjoyment from anyone—except, of course, unless it was a gay couple wanting to get married. Louisiana, independent and Bible-belt fearless to the end, one of the last strongholds against marriage equality, hadn't even given in immediately to the federal law passed in 2015; it had to be forced. I could hear the South's slow, rich treacle-sweet cadence in Mike's voice, see the stubbornness born of generations of sparring for a place to call home, only to find that hard-won home rejects you. He'd moved to Massachusetts, I knew, that very year. Not just for a marriage; for a life.

"It was supposed to be forever," said Mike. "We laughed a lot together, ate too much popcorn at movies, took turns doing the laundry. And so when we finally had the chance to make it legal, we did it. It's something I'll never forget."

He fell silent, and I kept the images swirling in my head. I sometimes planned weddings for older—if not actually elderly—people, for people who had lived together faithfully and loved well for over sixty years before tying the knot. I still got teary-eyed about the whole thing.

"So what went wrong?" I asked quietly.

"Can't let the heteros have all the fun," he said lightly. "If they can divorce, then so can we."

Gallows humor. I waited.

He took a very deep breath. "He'd been itching to move to the west coast. We thought it was a sign: you know, get married, have a new life. We could buy a house, maybe down the road adopt a child." Um, no, knowing Mike, probably not, but I let that one go. "Austin did film studies in college, and even though he'd been working for some computer company, what he really wanted was to be part of the movie scene. Part of Hollywood." He shrugged; he wasn't looking at me again.

"How long?"

He didn't pretend to misunderstand me. "It was a fairytale really, wasn't it? At least for him. La-la land. He landed a job almost as soon as we hit LA. He didn't have to spend years waiting, inching his way up; he produced some low-budget film about a kid who grows up with same-sex parents, and it exploded at Cannes and Toronto. He didn't even try the fringe festivals, Dublin and Edinburgh, just went right to the top. He was a producer. He was happy."

"You, on the other hand…"

"Ah, yes. Me, on the other hand." He gave a mirthless laugh. "I got to be night manager at a Marriott Hotel. And suddenly it seemed there wasn't time for anything. I was on nights; he filmed during the day. He traveled; most of the time he seemed to be traveling. All that shit we used to do together—poof. Gone. We kept it together for about six months and then he was about to leave for Vancouver for a shoot and I told him if he went, I wouldn't be there when he came back. Said I had to re-assess what it meant to me for him to pursue a career that didn't include me in his life."

"What happened then?"

"He offered me a job. Assistant to the prop manager."

There was a moment of silence. "You came back east," I said finally.

He nodded. "I came back east." Dragging the corpse of his dead marriage with him. The coffin's lid could be nailed down—or screwed down, one small bit of arcane knowledge—later.

"Have you seen him since?"

Mike was watching the napkin, twisted in his hands. "Never," he said. "Do-it-Yourself divorce kit online. He did invite me to his second wedding a couple of years ago, believe it or not, but I found I was required elsewhere."

"And now he's here," I said. "With his new husband?"

"Doubtful." Mike shook his head. "Unless the guy wanted to be assistant props manager."

"There's that," I agreed. He was looking haggard and older than he was supposed to look. He still loved this idiot. Oh, Mike. "Seriously, go home. There's nothing going on here today Glenn and I can't handle. You don't have to worry about running into this guy."

He stood up, put his chair back on top of the table, cleared his throat. "It's all right," he said. It wasn't. But it also wasn't any of my business.

And I had a wedding to set up.

Ali was irritated with me, there was a woman who'd died at Whaler's Wharf, Mirela was going back to Bulgaria to maybe become a mother to someone else's kid, my manager was heartsick, and the wedding of arguably America's Most Famous Actor was impending. You could say I had a lot on my mind.

So, naturally, that was when my mother called.

***

She has an unerring sense of timing, I'll give her that. *Bad* timing.

"I thought you'd want to know about Eileen and Mitchell," she was saying. "Since you're into weddings and everything."

She made it sound like crashing them was my hobby. "I'm not *into* weddings," I said. "They're my *job*." And who the hell were Eileen and Mitchell?

"Well, for someone who hasn't had one of her own, you go to a lot of them," my mother said.

Breathe, Riley, I counseled myself. *Just breathe.* I counted to five, which was about all I could muster given the day. "Ma, what's up? I have work to do."

"That's what you always say." A long sigh. My Mother the Martyr. "I haven't seen you since Christmas when we came to your lovely inn," she said.

"Yeah, Ma, I know. I was there." Most of the time I'm able to keep my sarcasm in check. Except when I'm talking to my mother. Or to myself.

"Don't take that tone with me, Sydney," she said. "You know I don't like it when you take that tone."

Was there any point to this conversation? "Ma," I said, a little desperately, "have you heard of Brett Falcone?"

"Well, of course I've heard of Brett Falcone," she snapped. "Who hasn't heard of Brett Falcone? He was on the cover of E magazine last week. I saw it at the hairdresser's."

I had a sudden feeling I'd hit gold. My mother lives in a very upscale (some would say Stepford-esque) community in New Hampshire. The weekly hairdresser appointment was part of The Way Things Are Done. And I was handing her gossip for the next appointment on a silver platter. "Well, he's here," I said.

"Don't be ridiculous, Sydney. He lives in Hollywood."

"He may live in Hollywood, but tomorrow evening he's getting an award at the Province-town International Film Festival," I said. "And in about two hours, he's getting married at my inn."

Silence. I'd done it. I'd shut my mother up. The only other time I could remember doing anything similar was when I fell off the stage during a recital in third grade. It was a heady feeling.

More silence, and I started wondering if she might have passed out. I didn't want to be the one to give in first. I really didn't want to be the one to give in first.

I gave in. "Ma? Are you still there?"

"It's hard to believe you're serious," she said.

"I couldn't make this up," I assured her. "Which is why I have to get to work, Ma—"

"I'll need a picture," she said. She'd gone from put-upon parent to fangirl in about three seconds flat. I kind of liked the change.

"Sure thing, Ma."

"Signed."

"Yes, Ma."

"His wife, too."

Ah. Right. It had been too good to last. "He's marrying another man, Ma," I said. "But

63

don't worry, I'll get *his* autograph for you, too, if you want. He's a famous screenwriter."

Another silence. Okay, this really wasn't fun anymore. Finally she said, ""Why do you do that?"

"Do what?"

"Try to shock me."

Breathe, Riley. Just breathe. "Ma, I live in Provincetown. You've been here. I don't have to make up gay people to shock you. They're real."

"But—Brett Falcone! He's so famous! He's so handsome! That movie he was in, he had such great chemistry with the leading lady, what was her name? They were so romantic together!" My mother had just managed more exclamations in a single sentence than she generally allowed herself in a week. "Women just—I don't know, they *swoon* over him!"

Him, and every other young fit gay man, and there are a lot of them. "That's why they call it acting, Ma. He's good at it."

"Apparently so." She was digesting the information.

I didn't have time for it. "Ma, he's getting married today. Here. Soon. I really have to go."

And I still didn't know who Eileen and Mitchell were.

5

Ali and Mirela showed up together for the wedding. They could easily have been another Hollywood golden couple here for the film festival; they're both gorgeous on their own, Ali with his brooding dark good looks, Mirela sun-streaked blonde and curvaceous. Together, they're stunning. I could imagine festival-goers staring at them, trying to place them among the Beautiful People.

By that time, I was totally organized. Well, almost totally. Everything was set up on the outside patio, the bower interlaced with flowers and ribbons, the table ready for the sand ceremony the grooms had requested, the chairs all neatly lined up, the guests finally wandering out from the bar where they'd been downing aperitifs, chattering as they took their places. Glitterati, most of them. My mother would have been one of the swooning women she'd alluded to, for sure.

Brett and Justin appeared together, Gregg Peterson moving around them taking pictures. I'd been happy to snag Gregg for them. He's a fantastic wedding photographer but also, in my opinion, the World's Sweetest Man. They had their own photographer in residence for the rest of the week, of course. They were selling pictures to the tabloids. I'd been shocked the first time I realized people did that—I think it was Michael Douglas' wedding, when one of the People-type magazines paid as much for the photographs of the wedding as the couple had paid for the wedding itself. And it was one *hell* of a wedding. Rich people do things differently from the rest of us.

There was a ripple among the guests as Brett and Justin passed, smiles all around, as if the happiness of these two larger-than-life figures might somehow bestow itself on those they touched. Like stardust.

Ali has theories about people like Brett Falcone. Movie stars, he says, don't matter anymore. Financially, sociologically, culturally, they're either obsolete or doing a damn good job of pretending to be. Whether it's because they stopped doing what movie stars are supposed to do, or we stopped wanting them to do it, here we all are, apparently, in a *post-*movie-star universe in which the movies seem to be doing just fine without the presence of an entire category of people who have been, for the better part of the past century, the main reason a lot of people went to the movies.

And, he contends, we shouldn't be surprised if our primary allegiances are to genres and concepts and properties rather than to people. If our biggest modern movie stars are Batman and Bourne and Wolverine and James Bond, and if the most a flesh-and-blood actor can hope is to be chosen to serve as the temporary avatar for one of those characters, then what meaning can the term *movie star* possibly have?

When Ali talks like that, I point out that people like Brett Falcone, even when they deny it, still have star appeal. In fact, Ali is a big Falcone fan. He should be, I tell him, the first to recognize that we still need movie stars. And thank heavens we still *have* movie stars—lots of them, and arguably a more talented and interesting variety than at any time in the past thirty years. But they play by new rules, and they have to navigate an industry that often seems hostile to their very existence.

The harpist finished the processional, and Vernon Porter—resplendent in his alter persona of Lady Di, with rhinestones glittering and wearing the brightest lipstick I'd ever seen anywhere, began to officiate the service. "We are gathered here…"

I stood in the back and watched it all. Someone might need a tissue; the horrible child with the famous actress might need to be whisked off to the bathroom. Brett's personal assistant, Brian, had been firm. "Nothing," he said, "can be allowed to mar the moment."

I had stared at him. "Mar the moment? *Mar the moment?* Do people really talk like that in LA?"

"I do," he'd said. "Who cares about anyone else? And his agent is going to want more champagne tonight. I have a list of what he'll need. Shall we go over it now?"

Obnoxious little git.

He was there in the second row, looking smug and self-satisfied. The more people in this strange wedding party I met, the more I was convinced I never wanted to visit Hollywood. I was rapidly coming to the happy conclusion that I lived on the correct coast.

I went up when it was time for the sand ceremony, a curious ceremony-within-a-ceremony in which the couple pours two distinct colors of sand into a common vessel. "Just as these grains of sand can never be separated and poured again into the individual containers," intoned Lady Di, "so will your marriage be."

I personally wasn't so sure that a complete mingling of lives as to make the individuals indistinguishable was the most enlightened approach to marriage, but hey, I'm single, what do I know?

And then they got their blessing and declaration, the harpist started playing again, and the deed was done.

Not my deeds, of course. I still had to move the whole lot of them as gracefully as possible into the restaurant—closed this evening so they could enjoy themselves without fans staring—where Adrienne the diva chef had an amazing reception waiting. Martin, the maître d', winked at me as I herded them all in. "Having fun, are we?"

"Save your sarcasm," I said cheerfully. "They're your problem now." I went back to the patio to help fold chairs and clear the space—the swimming pool with its tiki bar is nearby, and guests traditionally like more space to congregate with their bright drinks—and found Mirela and Ali still there, deep in discussion.

"You're missing out on Adrienne's hors d'oeuvres," I remarked. It *was* remarkable: no one in their right mind misses out on anything from Adrienne the diva chef.

Ali held up his arm and when I approached him, slid it around my waist and then pulled me down into his lap. "Nice wedding, *cara*," he said. That was a good sign: if he was speaking Italian, then our little texting tiff must be over.

I kissed the top of his head. "Thanks."

Mirela sighed. "Ali thinks that I should not go home," she said.

"I didn't know you were collecting opinions," I said. "I'll second that emotion. You just can't leave P'town in the middle of the season."

"It is not the middle of the season," she pointed out.

"Even worse, then," I said. "You can't leave P'town at the *beginning* of the season." And I was right: we make our money, all of us, in the summer. Kids from Bulgaria come and sleep ten to a room and work three jobs, flying down Commercial Street on their bicycles as they race from one to the next. The tourist shops open and start selling small objects that have the magical words "Cape Cod" on them in some form or another. Restaurants start being firm about reservations, inns are going full throttle, and the art galleries—and there are a lot of them, we're the oldest continuously operating art colony in America—find new patrons and welcome the old back.

Relevant, of course, because Mirela was an artist.

She was shaking her head. "This is my family," she said. "You cannot say no to your family."

Try mine, if you want practice saying no, I thought grimly. "Why suddenly now?" I asked instead. "You've never ever talked about your family, Mirela. Never. And now it's so important you have to go back to Bulgaria and maybe get stuck there?" That was me voicing my own fears, but that knowledge didn't slow me down. "What if you find you can't come home—come back, I mean?"

"Which one is home?" Ali asked her, unerringly and directly putting his finger on the problem. "My parents have always struggled, even after so many decades here, to figure out

73

whether it's the United States or Lebanon that's home for them."

She had told me she had to go "home." I hadn't really thought much about the language aspect of the statement at the time. Ali seemed to find it significant.

Mirela was shrugging. "I do not know," she said. "Perhaps that is my problem. I have chosen a life here, yes? But the pull from my family, it is strong."

"Strong enough to change your whole life around?" I asked. "Mirela, are you seriously considering raising a child by yourself?"

Wrong question; I could see it in her eyes. "If I am here, yes! Then I am alone, I am by myself, as you say it!" she snapped. "You are right. In Bulgaria, there are many people to help raise a child. I will not be alone in Bulgaria. Maybe this is what answers Ali's question."

"Oh, hell." I slid off Ali's lap and into a chair adjacent to Mirela. I reached over and took her hand. "You know there are people here who love you," I said.

"Who?" She was still upset. "Guy? He said he would be here, and here is where he is not!"

I'd wondered when the name of Guy Husband, English adventurer and one-time Mirela flame, would come up again. And I wasn't terribly surprised at the context. I'd never pegged him for anyone who would stay around for anything, despite the enticement of Mirela's beauty, and especially not if someone else's baby needed its diaper changed. I was tense enough to say what I was thinking. "He finds shipwrecks for a living, Mirela. He's not going to settle down." *Good job, Riley: state the obvious. Tell her that her love was lying to her from the start.* "And we love you. A lot of people in P'town love you."

It was too little, too late: I could see it in her eyes.

Ali cleared his throat. "Why don't we go to the party," he suggested, his voice gentle. "There's time to talk about this later."

"Is there?" Her chin was out, assertive, demanding. "Is there time?"

I saw it then. "You already have your ticket," I said, my voice flat. "You know when you're leaving."

Mirela nodded. "Tomorrow," she said.

Ali shot me an agonized look, but I was tired and more than a little scared about what this all was going to mean for us. I stood up. "Well, I have to go," I said. "Make sure you say good-bye before you leave." And don't, as my mother would have said, let the door hit you on your way out.

Okay, so maybe I was being unreasonable. But Mirela was my closest friend. She was the one I turned to with everything, joy or disaster, stupid questions and stupider comments. I didn't know how I could handle her going back to Bulgaria and never coming home again. If that doesn't make you unreasonable, what would?

Back at the reception, everyone who was anyone was having a blast. Music. Champagne and bright cocktail concoctions. Adrienne the diva chef's fantastic food.

Martin and Mike stood together at the back of the room, surveying the party. "Is he here?" I asked Mike.

He nodded. "Guy over there," he said, pointing the man out with a discreet gesture. "Gray suit, scarlet tie."

"The one with the *soul patch*?"

"That's what *I* said, honey," Martin put in. "I told Mike he's so much better off without having to look at *that* every morning. Talk about *retro*! Honey, the nineties called, and they want their facial hair back!"

"Hey now, you're an all-star, get your game on, go play," I sang. I'm no slouch when it comes to the right song for the right occasion.

"You are both so full of it," said Mike, but he said it without heat. Maybe he was healing. "Nice wedding, Sydney."

"Glad it's behind us," I admitted. "Now we can relax and just do the festival."

In that prediction, as in most things, I was proved to be stunningly wrong. But only in a way.

***

Julie Agassi was waiting for me at the front desk. "We need you to sign some paperwork," she said. "And I knew how ridiculous it would be for me to ask you to come to the police station and then actually expect you to appear."

"It's the season," I said, just as she added, completely in synch, "I know, I know, it's the season."

"So what happened?" I asked. "This is about the woman at Whaler's Wharf, isn't it?"

"Unless you've come across another homicide since then you haven't told me about," she said drily. "Which I wouldn't put past you.

Sydney Riley is to dead bodies as a pig is to truffles."

"Now *there's* an image that isn't going away anytime soon," I said. She'd opened a folder and pulled out a piece of paper. "Your statement," she said. "Read it through and sign it if you agree."

"I took it from her and started to read. "I didn't know I'd made a statement."

"I took the liberty," she said. "The DA's office wants to move this along."

"The DA's office?" I looked at her sharply. "Then it definitely *is* murder?"

She shrugged. "You saw her neck," she said. And I had: the bruising had been obvious, even to me, even in just those few seconds. Ligature strangulation, I think they call it. "Just sign the damned paper, Riley, won't you?"

I signed the damned paper and held it out to her. "Any motive?" I asked. "Any suspects?" I may be great at Smashmouth; I'm even better at Clue.

"You think the Staties share their opinions with me?" She took the paper and slid it into her folder. It was a definite sore spot. Local police can assist the state police in the investigation; they're never in charge of it.

"I assume that's a rhetorical question," I said.

She nodded. "They're all over this. As are a couple of people from the DA's office," she said, and shrugged. "You ask me, they're psyched to be here when there are so many movie stars in town. Who doesn't want to rub elbows with the great and the good?"

I assumed that was rhetorical, too. "They'll turn the film festival into a circus," I predicted.

"Anything to get a Brett Falcone autograph," agreed Julie. She shrugged again. "Ah, well. As you are constantly pointing out, it's the Silly Season. And it's only just begun." She glanced at my face. "Hey. Try and keep the body count down this year, will you, Riley?"

I made a face. "Honestly, Julie, I'm surprised you haven't locked me up yet, the rate you keep blaming me for finding dead people." The very thought sent a shiver down my spine. I'd spent far too much time at the police station during a different Silly Season, when they thought Ali had tried to blow up a float at Carnival. I had no wish to reacquaint myself with the station's dismal interior architecture.

"I'm working on it," said Julie. She looked past me toward the closed doors of the dining-room. "Wedding go okay? She was supposed to be part of it, wasn't she, this Caroline Cooper?"

"Yeah." I'd only learned that at the last minute myself, when one bridesmaid too few showed up in the lineup. It was interesting, since the grooms had made it a point to tell me she *hadn't* been here just for the wedding. Brett had said a word about Caroline's absence at the reception, just before the toast. Everyone accorded her a solemn twenty seconds of respect, before cheering the couple; the toasts continued for some time, everyone wanting to make their wishes known, especially in front of the photographers. Life, apparently, went on, bodies in bathrooms notwithstanding. "*They* won't find out who did it," I said suddenly, turning to face Julie.

"Oh, no, you don't." She was already backing up.

"Listen," I said, as persuasively as I could. "No one's going to talk to the Staties, or anyone from the DA, not these people, and you know it. They come from a place where they eat attorneys for breakfast. But I'm already here, I'm on the inside, they'll talk to me."

"You listen to me, Riley." Her cheeks were slightly flushed; I'd gotten under her skin.

"This isn't a game. You're not Miss Marple and you're not Jessica Fletcher. This is a woman's life, a real woman who had a family, who had friends, who had a career. You can show some respect for it by backing off." She paused. "I mean it, Sydney."

"Yeah, yeah, yeah." I flapped my hand at her, knowing it would drive her ballistic. "Scout's honor, officer."

"Detective," she corrected me.

"Whatever," I said. "Mark my words: these people are closing ranks. They think of all of us as lesser human beings. You know what the film society's like. So don't forget when they come up with nothing that I could have been useful." Why in the hell were these words coming out of my mouth? It wasn't as if I had nothing to do all week. And she was right: I wasn't a detective, I didn't even play one on TV.

But she was wrong about one thing: I did know Caroline had had a life. Every single time I got involved in some kind of police matter (and how's that for a euphemism for murder?), I felt nothing but respect for the victim, respect and outrage—that someone had decided they didn't have the right to go on living. There's unfairness everywhere in the world, but somehow murder seems worse than the rest of it. My life is so much more important than your life, so much so that if you threaten me or my family or my comfort in any way, I can just *end* you. There's something so primitively wrong about that… who doesn't want to see justice done? And if you can help, why wouldn't you?

I didn't say any of that to Julie. She was unhappy enough with me as it was.

Julie put the folder into her briefcase and snapped it shut. "I mean it," she said. "You're busy with the film festival; stay busy with it. Don't step on anybody's toes." She turned back at the door. "I mean it. Are we on the same page?"

"I got it," I assured her. But I somehow didn't think this was over. Whatever had been started here, the body in the bathroom hadn't ended it.

6

The next night proved me right.

It didn't feel like all hell was going to break loose when the day started, of course. I woke up with Ali asleep on one side of me and Ibsen on the other, aware that it was hot and sticky, and that I had an afternoon tea for the film festival I was going to need to oversee. And that Mirela might or might not be leaving town.

Okay, so it wasn't a particularly *joyous* awakening, but I never thought things would go as far off the rails as they did.

Ali was dead to the world; he used to be in some secret specialized group in the military and can fall asleep on a dime—*and* sleep the sleep of the righteous. I'm the one who needs Ambien. I got out of bed and put myself under the shower to try and get rid of the feeling of mild apprehension in my stomach. Mirela was going to be all right. Mirela was going to come back. Of course she was.

I put on my summer uniform of flowery dress and flat shoes, my hair caught up in a ponytail. One thing I had to do today was get that damned autograph for my mother, or I'd never hear the end of it all.

Ali was driving Mirela up to Boston to catch her plane. We'd argued about it the night before, of course. "That's absurd! She can afford Cape Air!"

"It's not what she can afford, it's what friends do for each other."

"And I suppose it never occurred to you to ask me if you could take the Little Green Car?"

"That's what *partners* do for each other," he said.

I gritted my teeth. I hate the term "partners." Yeah, it works, since we don't have a better word, and having a "boyfriend" when I'm in my mid-thirties does seem slightly juvenile; but partners always sounds to me like we're sitting in a boardroom somewhere. "Seriously, I don't know why you're encouraging this," I said.

"Because it's what Mirela wants."

I didn't have an answer for that, so I fell back on blaming the season. "It's going to take you two or three hours to get off the Cape, and more than that to get back on," I said.

"I have the time." He was infuriatingly calm, and I liked him a lot in that moment. I didn't *like* liking him a lot, though, and I was feeling somehow thwarted, though I didn't know why.

"Fine." I'd said it deliberately, the way women tell men things are fine when they are clearly anything but. And now this morning I was regretting the words, regretting behaving like that. What was it my mother was always saying? Don't take that tone with me?

I thought about waking him and apologizing, but in the end decided it wasn't going to help. I was still going to feel unhappy about the whole Mirela-going-away thing, and he was still going to believe I wasn't being supportive enough. So I took myself off to work.

Brett and Justin were in reception when I arrived at the inn, talking with Glenn. "Congratulations," I said to them as I slipped back behind the desk into the cubby-space I like to think of as my office.

"Sydney! It was perfect!" exclaimed Brett. "We couldn't have asked for anything that beautiful." Well, they *had* asked for doves, but I didn't feel a need to remind them of that. "I'm glad," I said. Later, I'd ask them for a testimonial: it wouldn't hurt to have Brett Falcone singing the praises of the Race Point Inn. "What's on your dance card for today?"

Justin's smile couldn't have gotten any bigger. "Brett's award," he said.

Glenn looked interested. "What award is that?"

"It's a special one the film society is giving Brett," Justin said. "For lifetime achievement."

Lifetime achievement? He wasn't a day over forty. But I smiled. "Then congratulations, again," I said.

Justin was in a chatty mood. "They're doing the ceremony this afternoon at Town Hall," he said. "Then a small cocktail party for donors at Water's Edge Cinema."

"Fitting it in between the afternoon screenings and the evening ones," Brett put in. Well, that made sense: the week was all about the films. "Why don't you both come? As my guests?"

I started to make an excuse when Glenn said, smoothly, "That would be fantastic. We'd love to come."

Okay. I managed another smile. We had a cocktail party at the inn, too, but if my boss wanted me over at Whaler's Wharf instead, to Whaler's Wharf I'd go.

Glenn watched them leave with a benevolent smile and caught my look. "They're good for business," he said.

"I know." And I did; I was just feeling a little overwhelmed.

I'd barely started checking my email when someone else came up to the desk. Glenn had left and I had no idea who was supposed to be there now. I sighed, got up, and turned around to help whoever it was. He looked awfully familiar.

"Sandy? That's your name, right? Sandy?"

"Sydney," I said. "I'm sorry, I should remember yours—"

He didn't wait for me to embarrass myself any further. "I'm Jack Donnelly," he said. "We met at breakfast yesterday."

"Of course." I really should pay more attention to guests. "How can I help you?"

He glanced left and right and lowered his voice to conspirator level. "Any chance you can get us tickets to that special award ceremony this afternoon? You must be in the know."

I laughed; I couldn't help it. "I'm a lot less important than that," I said. "But Brett and Justin just left—you might be able to catch them out on Commercial Street."

"No, no, wouldn't want to bother them," he said. "We can always buy the tickets—but you know us newshounds, always looking for what we can get for free."

"Do you do this a lot?" I asked. "Go to film festivals, report on them?"

"Irene does," he said. "Remember Irene? From breakfast? I knew her, back in the day." That's right; he'd worked for some publication that had apparently gone belly-up. "When I came back, it was like I'd never left. I still have the eye. You have to have the eye. You have to know what makes a movie a great movie." He leaned further against the counter, happy to chat, nothing on his mind. "You know what it really is? I decided I wanted to spend my life doing something important, something I love."

"Film festivals?"

He nodded. "Film festivals," he said.

It takes all kinds, I thought. And maybe going around to film festivals and writing about them *was* important work; who can say? "Do you live in Los Angeles?" I asked.

"Oh, God, no," Jack said and laughed. "I'm not nearly hip enough for that. Besides, all these films, you know, indie films, art films, they're getting made everywhere now. The Midwest, even, if you can believe that. No, I live in Boston."

"Are there indie films made in Boston?" I asked curiously. I spend a fair amount of time in Boston myself, what with my *partner* living and working there. I wondered if I should tell Jack that Ali's sister was the Boston police commissioner, give myself a little street cred. Probably not.

"There are indie films everywhere," he said again. "Boston in particular, even. It's such a great city. Picturesque. I wouldn't live anywhere else. I hated being away, you know, and now that I'm back, I'm never leaving. And there's a great film festival in Boston every year, you know. You should come to that." He grinned. "The BFF," he said.

I looked at him blankly.

"You know, BFF," he said. "Best friends forever? Boston Film Festival?"

My phone bleeped to indicate the arrival of a text. Jack saw me glance down and said, quickly, "Well, I won't keep you. I'll see you around, Cindy."

"See you." I couldn't be bothered to correct him; I'd seen who the text was from and clicked through. It was Ali. *Leaving to take Mirela to airport.*

I texted back, fast. *Wait. I want to say goodbye.*

We're outside.

I jammed my phone back into my pocket and headed out. The Little Green Car—my ancient Honda Civic—was idling at the curb, Ali behind the wheel, Mirela out and leaning against it. "Sunshine," she said to me by way of greeting.

"Mirela." I enveloped her in a hug. "I wish there were more time—"

She shook her head. "It is fine. It is easier like this."

I searched her face. "You *are* coming back, right? You have to come back. P'town won't be the same without you." And that was true; Mirela was part of my life nearly every day. It was unimaginable that she shouldn't be here. "Mirela, tell me you're coming back."

"I will email you when I arrive," she said, not answering my question.

A parking enforcement car pulled up behind them, and Ali leaned across the seat. "We have to go," he said. "See you tonight, Syd-ney."

Mirela gave me another hug and jumped in beside him. "Travel safely," I said automat-ically, not even knowing which of them I was saying it to, and after they'd gone I stared up the street after them, not even seeing the lan-yards and the colors, not even hearing the chatter of a warm June morning. It felt as if something seismic was happening, the earth moving below my feet.

I didn't like it. Not even a little bit.

***

By afternoon I'd more or less shaken the feeling of impending doom and was dealing with more prosaic problems. Glenn scooped me up a little before three. "Time to go see Brett get his award," he said.

"Already?"

"Come on. It'll be good for you to get out of the inn. Get some sun. See the people."

"I see people with lanyards," I said with a smile, imitating the I-see-dead-people trope from *The Sixth Sense,* one movie that *wouldn't* be playing at Water's Edge Cinema this week.

Town Hall was full; if I'd ever doubted Brett's star-power, I wouldn't anymore. The balconies were full. The oh-my-goodness-uncomfortable hard seats on the main floor were full. A big screen was lowered over the stage and clips of Brett's greatest hits scenes were played.

Gretchen came out and spoke at length about his contributions to international art films that went alongside his leading-man roles in blockbuster movies. "Brett Falcone is one of the few stars who bring quality acting to both venues, to both the commercial and the artistic arenas, and we're especially proud to announce that after the reception, you can all come back here for a special screening of *Revenge,* his most recent movie and the pride of this year's Provincetown International Film Festival." She paused for applause. "And we're especially proud that Brett chose Provincetown to tie the knot yesterday with his *husband*, Justin Braden!" More applause. No mention of what had happened the night before that, and for a moment I wondered again about the woman who'd been strangled in the bathroom. I'd be back at Whaler's Wharf when this thing wrapped up; I wondered if there was anything left there to sleuth. I wondered if any of the artisans had seen Caroline Cooper before she'd become a dead body. I wondered if I could ditch the reception to try and find out.

Gretchen was winding down. "So without any further ado, I want to introduce Henry Beckham, who gave Brett his first role in *Crazy Little Liars* and is here to celebrate his lifetime achievement!"

Tentative applause; they'd been expecting Brett. An older man in a smart tuxedo came out on stage and gave Gretchen air-kisses before taking the microphone. "I know you're not here to listen to me," he started, an opening that pretty much guaranteed that we were going to have to listen to him. A long-winded story about picking Brett out of the gaggle of handsome young men waiting tables in LA and waiting for their big break. How Brett had been a natural. How proud he, Henry, was to be able to be here today.

And then finally Brett came out and suddenly the house was on its feet, thunderous applause that went on and on and on. He had to try to talk over it twice before the audience finally subsided, sitting down, nudging each other.

He wasn't just a star; he was their star. I glanced at Glenn, whose eyes mirrored the excitement around us. *Our* star, I amended my thought.

Gretchen re-appeared, lugging rather than carrying the special trophy; it had a solid base topped with a star—what else?—and looked heavy. Better her than me, I thought inconsequentially; I'd probably have dropped the damned thing. She and Brett air-kissed and she handed him the trophy. It was heavy, all right. He turned to face the hall, lifting it aloft with just a touch of obvious effort, and the applause came again.

"I can't tell you how much this means to me," he said finally, when the room had quieted down. "I've been thinking a lot lately about this business, about being what they call a movie star, a leading man, whatever, and I know that's more about you than it is about me. Being a movie star is an unteachable quality that involves being someone the audience gets emotionally invested in, regardless of the material. We all go to the movies to see heroes doing heroic things. You do it, I do it. The emphasis on actors being able to singlehandedly open, or carry, or rescue a movie seems like an extension of that wish. To equate stardom with mere bankability ruins the fun."

He paused. "*Revenge* is a great movie, not just because I'm starring in it—though I'd like to think that's part of the fun!"—everyone gave an obliging laugh—"but because of the great people behind it, and I just want to single out two of them today. The first is the person Gretchen just alluded to, and that's my—can you believe it? brand-new husband, Justin Braden." Another pause, and applause broke out again. When it had quieted down, Brett continued. "The other person is one-half of a fabulous production team that made *Revenge* possible, and unfortunately she can't be here with us today. I'm talking about Caroline Cooper, and she was killed right here in Provincetown two nights ago, by person or persons still unknown." A shiver ran around the room, hushed exclamations. The trite phrase seemed something of a rebuke. I shifted in my chair, uncomfortable, as though he'd pointed to me and added, *And Sydney Riley found her body!* I glanced around to make sure that part was all in my head.

"So I want you all to come back this evening and watch *Revenge,* which is Caroline's finest work ever, and I want you to do it for me, and for Justin, and for her. Right now we have to go over to Whaler's Wharf for something, but we'll be back, and I've made sure we're offering the viewing free of charge to the public, so make sure you're on time!" There was another slight stir, restless: festival pass-holders were special, and here he was equating them with the *hoi polloi*. Brett sailed over it. "We want Caroline's last film to be her crowning triumph," he said. "And I have to say—it means a lot to me and Justin that you're here, that you're celebrating this film, that we were able to make our special day part of this whole special week. This award is the only thing that could have made things more perfect for me, and all I can say is… thank you!" He raised his voice. "We love you, Provincetown International Film Festival!"

Whew. Glenn and I ducked out as the applause started again. "Seriously—do we have to go to this cocktail party?" I asked. "I've got something at the inn—"

"Mike will take care of it," said Glenn. I stared at him. "You're as much under his spell as Ali," I said. Ali had called me from Logan Airport where he'd dropped Mirela off; his main desire being to make it back in time for the cocktail party I was trying to get out of. He was welcome to it. I personally was fine not seeing any more of the golden couple; I'd crossed them off my checklist and had other pressing items on it. "Seriously. Look at yourself! You guys are like giggling teenage girls."

"Really?" He looked at me and smiled, and I had to smile in return. Glenn is a bear—large, hairy, very much the physical opposite of an adolescent girl. But totally adorable in his own way.

"Okay, okay, let's go to the reception," I said, linking my arm through his. "Why the hell not."

Once we got to Whaler's Wharf, we were, of course, the first ones there. Glenn spied a friend and fellow bear and was quickly deep in conversation, so I decided to wander a bit. It was moving up to dinner time, at least for the tourists, and the open-air interior of the building was pleasant, a breeze coming off the harbor sweeping through the interior. Mind you, that same wind whistles a lot more aggressively through the space in the winter, but today it was gentle and somehow soothing.

I was about to go into one of the shops when, for the second time that day, Jack Donnelly suddenly cornered me. This time he was with his sidekick, Irene. For two people who—if I was remembering correctly—were catty with each other, they did seem to spend a lot of time together. "Hey, there! Girl from the Race Point? Are you following us?"

"Hi, Jack." At least this time I remembered his name, and he had fortunately not attempted mine. "Hi, Irene."

She was craning her neck, looking up the two additional floors that looked for all the world like balconies. "This place is so cool," she said. "But it's not really a wharf, is it? I mean, it's just a building. How did it get designed like this?"

I knew what they wanted, and what the hell, I had to wait around for Brett and Justin and Ali anyway. And (as my boss always reminds me), hospitality is my middle name. "It started out as a wharf," I said, settling into my tour-guide persona. I do this stuff well. "Literally for whalers. Provincetown was once one of the whaling capitals of New England. And then eventually the industry died out, and sometime later the building became a movie house." This part was cool; I wasn't crazy about our whaling past, let's move along. "It opened in 1919 and was amazing—you have to think, everything else in town was built of wood, but here's suddenly this huge place built of stone. It was a statement. It was called the Provincetown Theater, and there was a big arch out front chiseled with the words."

I gestured toward the harbor end of the building. "Walk down here with me and I'll show you something," I said. We reached the rotunda with the fountain sparkling in the middle of it and took a seat on one of the benches, inexplicably unoccupied by tourists. "The 1960s and seventies were insane in P'town," I said. "There's a book out with Al Kaplan photographs, it's called *There Was Always a Place to Crash*, and that kind of says it all. Everyone open, everyone ready to do whatever. Not like these days, for sure." I gestured. "Whaler's Wharf got converted from the theater into an arts-and-crafts collective then. Early seventies, I think. Just down here, where the orchestra seating for the theater had been. But it was wild." I smiled; visitors always love this part. "The projectionist was a druggie, and people never knew what was going to happen. Once he even ran a whole film on the ceiling—and the audience put up with it."

"Sounds like quite a time," said Jack.

I nodded. "Then the theater closed in the eighties," I said. "They used the upper floors for storage. The shops endured, though, and rent was cheap, so artists could afford to work here." Not, I thought, like today. I didn't say it. No need to complain to the visitors. We did that all winter. "Then, just over twenty years ago, there was an electrical fire," I said. "People still talk about that fire. They thought it would take out the whole town. Firefighters came from all over the Cape, from the mainland. It destroyed Whaler's Wharf, and a good part of the Crown & Anchor next door."

"A lot going on over *there*," said Irene inconsequentially.

When it seemed she'd said everything she planned to say, I stood up. "Come back here," I said, and led them out the door onto the sand of the town beach. We were directly below the deck at Ross' Grill, and I had a quick shivery moment of memory. "That's what's left of the theater," I said, pointing out the broken-up chunks of the inscription from the arch of the façade, half-buried in the sand.

"Like a tombstone," said Irene.

"Not really," I said. "Check out the fat merman." Provincetown will never take itself *that* seriously.

Jack was looking up at Ross'. "That's something of a jump," he said. "Anyone ever get drunk and try it?"

"Not that I'm aware of," I said. "Listen, this is great, but I have to go." My conscience was catching up with me. What was wrong with this picture? I was supposed to be looking for clues, not playing tour guide to film critics.

"No problem," said Jack. He couldn't manage my name; I had a sudden impulse to call him Mack or Snack or something like that. *No time for snark, Sydney.*

I took the stairs that followed the rotunda up and around and paused outside Ross' Grill. But there wouldn't be anything left there to detect, and Caroline hadn't been strangled at the dinner table. I hurried along the second-floor passageway, glancing up and reminding myself guiltily that my accountant, Chip Capelli, was still waiting for my very extension-overdue taxes. Another day soon, I promised him silently.

Julie had confiscated my illegal bathroom key, and loitering on the landing outside the bathroom wasn't yielding much in terms of insights. I sat down on the top step and contemplated the place.

To be perfectly honest? If I were planning on killing someone, Whaler's Wharf would make a *terrific* choice for a venue. It's a warren of rooms within rooms, odd corners and little cul-de-sacs. Chip—a friend, I must say, as much as an accountant—had taken me on a tour once, down into the basement where renters keep items in storage cages and underground passageways run the length of the building. It's creepy, for sure, but surely not dangerous.

And, the truth was, Caroline hadn't been killed in the basement, her body stuffed into a cage (which is, truth be told, what *I* probably would have done with it, were I writing this story); she was in a bathroom she should have had no access to.

And I'd seen her neck. Strangled.

I sat and thought about it all some more, totally unproductively. There had to be something connecting all these thoughts. But I couldn't see it, and that was where I was still sitting when Ali found me. "There you are." He sat next to me, his elegant trousers on the grimy workaday staircase. I almost felt guilty. I had to get out of my own thoughts. "How's Mirela?"

He shrugged. "She's scared," he said. "She's happy, and she's afraid, and she's enthusiastic… I don't think she knows what to feel."

102

"I still don't see how this thing with her sister is her problem," I said.

"I think," said Ali carefully, "that she doesn't see how *you're* making it yours."

I stared at him for a moment, then burst out laughing. "Too right," I gasped, finally. "I'm still thinking the world revolves around Sydney Riley."

He gestured around the stairwell. "Playing detective?" he asked.

"Nothing to detect," I said. "I think it was probably easy. Not to get her here—I don't know about that part, except that it kind of points to it being someone she knew—but doing it? It was evening, the offices were empty, no one was around here. And I don't think it takes very long to strangle someone."

"They had to have a key," objected Ali. "You found her behind a locked door."

I sighed. "Yeah, there's always that, isn't there?"

He reached over and took my hand and kissed it. "Come on, Miss Marple," he said. "There's a movie star just around the corner waiting to give you a glass of champagne."

"I can't wait."

***

Ali got to stand in some pictures next to Brett, and the Beautiful People got to gossip together, and I got to drink too much champagne. Justin found me standing with my back to the wall and a completely inappropriate dreamy smile on my face. "Sydney."

"Hey." I tried pushing myself off the wall and then, when the room tilted slightly, decided not to. "That's some award."

"Sure is," he said.

There was a slight pause, which felt awkward. I cast around for something to say.

"So what's next for the two of you? After the festival, I mean?"

"We're heading up to Boston," he said. "My family's all there, and of course they *know* Brett, but we have to go and show off our wedding rings, maybe open some wedding presents. Then it's back home. I'm about six weeks behind on a screenplay, so no more partying for me for a while. I'll chain myself to my desk if I have to."

"I didn't know you were from Boston." My old hometown, too.

He nodded. "Got my MFA from BU," he said. "Took me over ten years to pay it off.

You know it's one of the most expensive schools in the country?"

"I didn't know that." Another long pause. Awkward. So much for my scintillating conversational skills. "But you like living in California?"

"Sure," he said. "Every day is summertime, every drive a traffic jam."

I laughed. "Like the Cape in season," I said.

"I'd noticed." He smiled. "I was last here, when was it? Twelve years ago? My mother was having surgery so I came back East to stay with them for a while, and my sister and I decided on a whim to visit P'town. I was all about flying in, Cape Air, you know, which is how I used to come when I visited, but she wanted to drive, wanted to go antiquing in Sandwich first. It was August." He paused. "It was appalling."

"Yeah, I can imagine." Route Six becomes a parking lot in the summer, and it's the only road in or out. "Did you make her drive back alone?"

"Should have, shouldn't I?" Something passed over his face, a memory perhaps, something dark. "Hell of a summer, that was. The whole time was horrible. I saw someone get killed." He looked at me. "Not like you and Caroline, though that's bad enough; I mean I actually saw it happen."

"How dreadful." The champagne was turning a little nasty on me. How many glasses had I drunk? "What happened? Was it a car crash?"

"No. That would've been easier. It was a stupid domestic situation, a couple, the guy shot his wife. On Commonwealth Avenue, right up near the Common." Some of the most expensive houses in the city, I was thinking, on an avenue designed by Hausmann. They say everyone in Boston eventually does time on Comm. Ave., but not generally at that end of it. "I was walking my mother's dog and we'd stopped for him to do his thing and I was just looking in lighted windows, the way one does, you know, when one's out at night like that. And I was standing there just looking into this apartment and saw him shoot her."

"Did he see you?"

He shook his head. "No, nothing like that. I was safe and all. Had to come back for the trial, of course." A rueful smile. "Didn't walk the dog anymore, though."

I shivered. "I'd think not."

"I write about all these convoluted murders," said Justin. "With deep motives and secret passions and all that, but in real life? Turns out, you know, most murders are either business-related—and I'm talking drugs and gangs here—or they're domestics that should never have happened. But you can't dress that shit up, can you?"

I remembered my thoughts after I'd seen Caroline. "Professor Plum in the library with the candlestick," I said.

"You got it."

Ali joined us. "*Cara*," he said, and kissed my cheek. He put his hand out to Justin. "Congratulations, man. Didn't get a chance to say so yesterday. It was a beautiful wedding."

"Thanks." Justin smiled. "Probably should go see what my better half's up to," he said. "Nice talking to you, Sydney."

"That looked serious," said Ali as the other man moved away.

I shivered. "Not really. Just conversation. I think I've had too much to drink."

He looked at me appraisingly. "You could be right. Too drunk to detect?"

"What are you talking about?"

"I just had a long conversation with Brett Falcone." He moved so he was standing beside me, his gaze sliding over the people in the room. Cops' eyes are never still. "He said Caroline was acting strange. She and Austin were arguing a lot—and apparently they never argue."

"Austin," I repeated. I'd just love it if Austin were the murderer. It would so serve him right for dumping Mike. "Did he tell Julie? Or the Staties?"

"He didn't want to steer them in any direction, but I think he's having second thoughts. He says in a town filled with odd people, Austin's odder than most. Listen, do you want me to call a cab? No way you're walking anywhere."

I looked at him blankly. "Are you going back to Town Hall? To watch *Revenge*?"

He shook his head. "I'll wait until it's on Netflix or Amazon," he said. "What *you* need is a quiet night at home."

That was what I thought, too. And while I was tottering up the stairs to my apartment, someone whacked Brett Falcone over the head with his shiny new award trophy and dumped his body in the sand in back of Whaler's Wharf.

7

J ulie Agassi called me the first thing in the morning. I swiped the phone screen a little blearily when I saw who it was; Julie isn't someone who calls just to chat. "Were you at the Water's Edge Cinema reception yesterday?" she demanded. "Someone said you were, but I didn't want to believe it."

"Why?" My head was hurting. Ibsen was purring next to me and it sounded like a freight train. I'd really only answered the phone to stop it ringing. "What's the trouble now?"

And then she told me.

"I was there, but I didn't see anything," I protested. "Ali and I left before anyone else, I think." I didn't add it was because I'd had too much champagne; Julie only drinks protein-powder smoothies. And I didn't like it that when anyone got killed I seemed to be her first port of call.

She probably felt the same way about me.

"Okay," she said. "Then do this for me. Give me a picture of these guys. You married them the other day, you should know them. Tell me about this wedding, about how they were together."

I struggled into a sitting position. Somehow it didn't seem respectful to be talking about sudden violent death when I was lying down. Even my pajamas somehow felt frivolous. "They're great together," I said automatically. "Totally fabulous. Why are you asking? Do you think the killer was at the wedding?" I closed my eyes and tried to visualize the wedding party, the guests. Too many people, most of them strangers to me, something of a blur. "I don't think I can help you there," I said.

"Okay," she said again. "When you left the party yesterday, what was going on?"

"I don't understand," I said. Beside me, Ali stirred and opened his eyes. "It's Julie," I told him. "Brett Falcone's dead." Something rose in my throat and I swallowed hard. I was *not* going to throw up. "He's been killed," I told Ali.

"What?" He went from sound asleep to completely awake in three seconds flat, the result of those years doing special missions in the military. Like a cat.

Julie was talking. "I did ask you a question," she reminded me. "What was going on at the reception?"

"What? Nothing," I said, and clicked my phone so she was on speaker. "It was a reception. People were drinking, people were talking, people were having their pictures taken. Brett was fine. I didn't see anyone—suspicious." But I'd been drinking, I wouldn't have thought a pink elephant in the room was suspicious. I've never been able to drink champagne gracefully, and this had been very good champagne. Ouch. "Ask Ali, he was there," I said.

"I'm here now," said Ali, up on one elbow. "Julie, what happened?"

"That's what I'm asking you," she said, a little grimly. "What happened at this party at the cinema? Did Falcone and Braden argue?"

It was a little jarring, her referring to Brett and Justin by their last names. "No, of course not," I said, just as Ali answered, "Not that I could see. No individuals were paying particular attention to either of them." Ali's in law

111

enforcement, too, and when he's in cop mode he and Julie share a language I find stilted and sometimes ridiculous. Today, it was scary.

"Okay," Julie said. "Thank you. We might have more questions later."

"Wait!" I yelped, and winced because even my own voice was too loud for my hangover. "Is this connected to Caroline Cooper?" It had to be; it was stretching credibility that two different killers with two different motives were stalking the same group of people. "Does it have to do with the movie?"

Ali was shaking his head. "She won't tell you," he muttered *sotto voce*.

But she did. "You might as well know," she said. "We've arrested Justin Braden. I'll be in touch." She clicked off, no doubt anticipating the torrent of questions I found myself aiming at a blank telephone screen. I looked at Ali. "This isn't happening," I said.

"It is," he said. He was already out of bed, pulling on a pair of jeans, sorting through the t-shirts in his carryall.

"Where are you going?" I demanded.

"To see if I can help."

"Why?" God, I sounded strident. "You work for ICE," I reminded him. And he does, though not in arresting immigrants; ICE also has a human trafficking department. Ali tries to make sure everyone who's in the country actually *wants* to be here.

"Because Justin needs someone there," he said.

"He needs an attorney, not an immigration investigator," I said. I was feeling awful, between Brett's being dead and Justin being accused and my head feeling like it might explode, and I have an unfortunate tendency to take that sort of thing out on my nearest and dearest.

Ali ignored my tone. "He needs a friend," he said. "Someone who knows the system." He was running his hands rapidly through his hair in lieu of combing it. He looked sultry and a little dangerous. "I'll catch you later," he said, already out the door. He has a morning efficiency I find depressing; this morning it seemed foreboding.

There was a war room going on at the inn when I got there. The front-desk kid—Peter? Paul? *Mary?*—told me they were in Glenn's office and expecting me.

I didn't bother knocking. It was that kind of day already.

The group inside was, perhaps predictably, all men. Glenn looked tired. I couldn't imagine how I looked. "Sydney," he said. "Come on in. We're talking about what happened."

"What *did* happen?" I demanded. "Does anyone really know? I can't believe Justin would kill Brett."

"Well, of course he wouldn't," said a guy in khakis and a polo shirt. Ralph Lauren, natch. I almost expected boat shoes. "This is Rob Francis," said Mike. "He's Justin's agent."

I didn't want to do the whole hand-shaking thing, and he seemed okay with nodding in my direction.

A slightly overweight Hispanic man in his fifties was in one of Glenn's guest chairs. "Miss Riley," he said. He was playing with an unlit cigar. "We met the other night at Ross' Grill." I had no recollection of it, but that didn't mean anything; something else had grabbed my attention. "And of course at the wedding." He lumbered to his feet, his hand out. The hand that had been holding the cigar. I shook it and felt faint. "Lou Estrada," he said. "I am—I was—Brett Falcone's agent.

There were two younger men who looked like production assistants just out of school or maybe even on college internships, and I let their names sail past me. Brian was there, of course, Brett's insipid annoying personal assistant. I wondered why he wasn't wherever Brett's body was at the moment. Didn't it have to go to the hospital first? There would be an autopsy. Why wasn't Brian personally assisting him there?

There was only one person left.

"And this is Austin Hyde," said Mike, his voice flat and emotionless. Mr. Soul Patch. "He and Caroline Cooper co-produced *Revenge*."

"So they did," I said. I hoped the expression I aimed at him was sufficiently frosty. I looked at Glenn. "The gang's all here, then?" It made sense: with the exception of the two kids, these were the moneymakers, the people behind the people on the screen. I wondered if Brett's death would help ticket sales. Probably.

"We have some attorneys joining us shortly," said Austin. His voice, I thought, went with his soul patch: thin and reedy and annoying. "They're coming down from Boston." That made sense, too: they needed someone admitted to the bar in the Commonwealth. For all I know, these people could well have someone they could call on in every state. And at this level of money and fame, the

mountain most definitely came to Moham-
med.

Austin sat down, uninvited, in Glenn's
other guest chair. "They didn't let me see Justin this morning, won't let anyone in but his
lawyer." He sounded astonished; there probably weren't a lot of doors slammed in his face.

I wondered fleetingly if that "not anyone"
included Ali, but on the whole assumed he'd
have been able to get in and talk to Justin. Law
enforcement sticks together, and by now the
Provincetown police department had a long
history with my boyfriend.

Much of it was even positive.

"Why do they think Justin did it?" I asked.
Might as well start from the beginning.

Lou looked sadly and longingly at his cigar
and didn't say anything. Rob let his breath out
in an explosive hiss but didn't say anything.
Mike seemed to be moderating the gathering,
anyway. "He was standing over the—um—"
He stopped himself. "Over Brett," he
amended belatedly and self-consciously.

"Where was this?"

"Out behind Whaler's Wharf. On the
beach. Where the broken-up sign is. You
know, the pieces from the old Provincetown
Theater—"

"I know," I cut in. Had it only been yesterday I'd been treating those same pieces of stone as an amusing tourist attraction? "Did he fall? From the restaurant?"

Austin said, his reedy voice cold, "He was hit over the head with his award trophy. And Justin was standing next to him, holding it."

I thought they were begging the question. And, besides, anyone who reads mystery novels knows it's not the guy standing over the body who did it. Duh. Then again, it was just possible that real life handled things differently. "How do we know it's the trophy he used?"

"Oh, for Christ's sake!" exploded Rob Francis. "It wasn't him. He didn't do it."

Mike said, "The trophy had blood on it. A lot of blood."

"And did Justin? You don't bludgeon someone to death and not share in the gore," I said. Lou shuddered theatrically.

Mike said, gently, "There was blood there, too."

There didn't seem to be anything to say to that, so I didn't say it. Took another tack instead. "When exactly did all this happen?" Water's Edge Cinema, where the cocktail party was being held, was on the street side of

Whaler's Wharf. You come in, you go upstairs, you don't go the length of the building. In fact, his death was the exact opposite of Caroline's: she'd been at a party on one end of the Wharf, her body found at the other end. Brett had been at a party at the end of the building where Caroline had ended up, and *his* body had ended up outside beyond Ross' Grill where she'd been at dinner. I had no idea if that meant anything, but it was sure symmetrical.

And there was a matter of timing: he had to leave the party to get back to Town Hall in time to introduce the movie screening. It was dusk, yeah, but still light enough to see.

I wondered, suddenly, what *Revenge*'s plotline was. I hadn't even seen any trailers, but then I'm more of a bookworm than a film buff. Surely it was irrelevant, anyway… right?

Rob was still spluttering. "There are about a million scenarios that could have ended in that scene," he said, using the group's familiar language. "The most likely is Justin saw it happen and rushed over to see if he could help Brett. They were newlyweds, for Christ's sake. Of course he'd try to help him."

"And picking up the trophy?" asked Austin, his tone disbelieving. "Getting *blood* on himself?" I decided that even if I hadn't disliked him before I met him, I was certainly disliking him now.

Rob waved the question off. "An automatic gesture," he said dismissively. "It's natural and human. We've seen it before. In *Driven*, when Sylvia Piccolo picks up the knife that just killed Adam Rogers—"

Lou looked up from his cigar-fondling. "You know that's a *movie* you're comparing this to, right?" he asked.

"Life imitating art," said Rob, shrugging, unconcerned. "It happens all the time."

I looked at Glenn and Mike, standing behind Glenn's desk as though it might protect them from Hollywood-itis. "Why didn't anyone see this happen?" I asked.

"We don't know that no one did," said Mike. He was looking steadily at Austin.

"The state police are here already," Glenn said to no one in particular. "Because of the— because of Ms. Cooper. I think they're probably making inquiries."

"They're going to need some reinforcements," I said, half under my breath. Once the high-powered lawyers got in from Boston, the DA's office was going to need all the help it could get.

"And in fact, they're staying here, at this inn, for Christ's sake," said Rob. "In the same hotel where Brett and Justin were staying!" He seemed to find the police presence personally insulting. Perhaps he'd have preferred to turn the inn into a shrine.

"We could make the space," said Glenn calmly. And we could; we always keep a few rooms in reserve. A room, a suite. Just in case. One of Glenn's dilemmas when he sent over-flow guests to the Crowne Pointe. Would he regret the empty rooms? The answer was, al-most never. "There's no reason to not accom-modate them."

And earn a little goodwill for the inn should it ever be needed, I thought. You could be sure the taxpayers of Massachusetts were footing the bill.

"Okay," I said. I pushed some papers back from the edge of Glenn's desk and sat on it, my back to my two bosses, and looked at the Los Angeles crew. I felt a little like a torch singer, spotlight in my eyes, getting ready to sing of something dark and lost and intense. "Were all of you at the party? The one at the cinema?"

"Who *are* you?" asked Austin, his voice strident. "Why should we tell you anything?"

"Sydney," said Mike evenly from behind me, "is accustomed to helping the police with their inquiries. She's an asset to the department. They rely on her." Well, maybe. Rely on me for something, anyway. Usually exasperation and entertainment. "She's probably our best chance of showing that Justin isn't guilty."

I ignored Austin. "So?"

We sorted out their answers. The two kids hadn't been there; they were both out and about on unspecified errands for the director, who wasn't *here* because he'd taken to his room this morning with a migraine. I could sympathize with that one. Brian, Brett's personal assistant, was at the cinema, but had left the party several times to take phone calls away from the noise.

Everyone else in the room, except Mike, had been there, but moving around, chatting, posing for photographs, getting another drink. "Well, for Christ's sake, of course we were there. We *have* to go," said Rob. "No one can miss it. It's like all the parties during the festival. That's half the job, being part of the scene, getting into the photos and the articles and the blogs."

I wasn't going to ask them how Brett and Justin had been behaving together; the police were hitting that angle first, if Julie's call was any indicator. Besides, I'd *seen* them. They were acting like a couple that just got married. They were behaving as if one of them had just been given a lifetime achievement award. I sat with the irony of that reflection for a moment—the lifetime achievement award had, after all, been given just in the nick of time—before marshalling my thoughts. "Okay. You all knew them both," I said. "Is there any *reason* you can think of for Justin to harm Brett? Any motive? Anything anyone can think of?"

"For Christ's sake—" Rob began, but Lou Estrada cut him off. "The money," he said.

I looked at him blankly. "What money?"

"The money Justin Braden inherits from Brett Falcone. With a bonus insurance clause, and the pay-out's a doozy. All thanks to being finally and legally married."

Brian and Rob started talking at the same time, their voices indignant. "He never would—" "That's irrelevant—" "Don't be ridiculous."

Lou was waving the cigar again. "It doesn't really matter," he said. "If Justin killed him for the money, he did it too soon."

That silenced them. "What are you talking about?" I asked.

Lou smiled, the cat who'd found the cream. "Because Brett hadn't changed his will yet. He was going to do it after everything— after the ceremony, after they went to Boston, after they got back to LA."

"Justin's his legal husband," I objected, shaking my head. "Even though the license hasn't gone through yet, as soon as Vernon— um, that's Lady Di, the officiant—as soon as Vernon declared them married, they were married. Doesn't he *automatically* inherit?"

"Not if someone else was already specifically named," said Lou comfortably. I wondered in passing whether that someone else might be him; he seemed to be enjoying himself far too much for a guy who'd just lost a client. Lou added, "And... someone was." He loved having a secret, knowing something his competitive colleagues didn't; you could just tell. "At best, what Justin would be looking at is a protracted legal battle. He'd end up with a lot of it, of course. Just not all of it."

"Who's inheriting, then?" Rob asked.

"I have no idea," said Lou blandly. Too blandly. "The point is, the money's not, as you tried to suggest, irrelevant. There will be enough to afford flowers for the funeral, and a nice send-off afterward, don't worry about that."

Money's never irrelevant, I thought. As the incredibly rich can tell you, you can never have enough of it. I'm among the forty percent of Americans who live one paycheck from disaster, so it's way relevant to me; but it's relevant to these people in a completely different way.

Still, I like to think I have a sense of people, of what they're like and what they might and might not do, and I just didn't see Justin killing Brett. Not for money. Maybe he could kill for passion, in the heat of a moment; I actually think any one of us could do that. But for gain? I'd seen how he looked at Brett during the wedding ceremony. And at the cocktail party, how even as we were chatting—God, about a different murder, talk about life imitating art or something like that—his eyes kept wandering, seeking out Brett, reaching out for connection, that same look of affection. They were like puppies together. Puppies don't kill each other.

Brian the obnoxious personal assistant obnoxiously cleared his throat. "There was," he said diffidently, "an old boyfriend."

"What are you talking about?" That was Austin, scowling at him. Austin didn't want to know about old boyfriends, not in this room. Brian's expression didn't change. I might not like the kid, but he had guts to say something unpopular in this group. After all, he was probably counting on one of the agents to get him his next gig.

"Brett used to know a guy here in Provincetown," said Brian. "Justin didn't want him at the wedding. He didn't want Brett to see him."

I turned so I could catch Mike's eye. Seemed like everyone in this story had some old romance catching up to them. Mike was watching Austin, but he was looking uneasy, some undercurrent there. I wondered if I should wonder why.

"Who?" Austin, again, peremptory.

That was, apparently, the end of Brian's information. "I don't know his name," he confessed. "I just know they went at it a couple of times before we left California. They were both talking about Brett having one last fling. Justin thought he was going to do it."

"And Brett?"

The kid shook his head. "I don't know," he said. "But... well, it wouldn't have been the first time he saw someone else since him and Justin got together."

Oh, great. The plot thickens even more.

I thought about it. Sometimes events come about, things happen, that grow organically from the soil of a place. There's a seed that moves its way through the earth and up into the air and light, and it's clear that particular plant couldn't, wouldn't, have grown anywhere else. It belongs. It might pollinate the garden or it might strangle it, but it is tied to the locus.

And then there are seeds brought in, ready to sprout, that need only a new home, a new place, a new locus to survive. When my boss Barry was murdered, the crime had been a Provincetown one: his killer's intent and actions all grew here, in the sea air and sun and salt of Land's End.

But this… I could feel this crime wasn't ours. That it didn't belong here. Dark thoughts, jealousies, frustrations, all these shadowed intentions had been nurtured somewhere else. They were brought to fruition in our town, in our moment; but they didn't belong to us.

Which made solving the crimes even more difficult, of course.

I sighed.

"So what are we going to do?" demanded Rob Francis, picking up on the sigh and teetering just this side of belligerent. "They say you're Miss Crime-Stopper, so what's the plan? Because, and maybe you don't realize this, but I gotta tell you, I'm not having my guy stay one more minute in jail than he has to. And if the police aren't gonna figure that out, then we have to do something. He may not be the star in this story, but he's valuable property. He can't be locked up."

"Although," mused Lou, apparently addressing himself to his cigar, "the publicity won't do him any harm."

Rob rounded on him. "What the fuck did you just say?"

Lou rolled the cigar delicately between his thumb and index finger. "Don't kid yourself," he said. "Seriously. Don't look now, we're already on CNN, on MSNBC, on all the cable channels, even on Fox. By this time next week it's the cover of People and E magazines. No matter what else happens, you just got your boy a ton of free publicity." He stretched his legs out in front of him. "It's that most delicious of gossip fodder: you've got love, gay politics, marriage, and murder all rolled into one. You couldn't pay for this kind of publicity."

"And that'll be just great," countered Rob, "assuming he doesn't end up convicted. What happens then, huh? They sent Aaron Hernandez to jail, didn't they? And you saw how that ended! The world forgot all about him until he topped himself."

I shivered at the reminder, though the air conditioning was barely running. No one in their right mind would consider publicity a good enough reason to go to Sousa-Baranowski, Massachusetts' only super-max prison. Once the former football star had realized he was there for good, he'd hanged himself in his cell. I didn't wish that place on anyone, and certainly no one as nice as Justin seemed to be.

For all his obnoxiousness, Rob was right. Justin couldn't have done this. Not to anyone, but especially not to his husband. I remembered the pain in his voice when he told me about once witnessing someone get killed. His compassion. And he was supposed to have turned around and in the following hour done the same thing to his new husband? I'm not *always* the world's best judge of human nature—some of my old boyfriends can attest to that—but I couldn't be that far off.

Lou was looking benignly at Rob. "Well, look at it this way, it got Hernandez a lot of publicity, didn't it? Didn't hurt the Patriots either, no matter how many crocodile tears Robert Kraft cried." He shook his head and, sadly it seemed, put the cigar into his pocket. "Of course, it's not quite the same thing, is it? Hernandez was a tight end on a winning football team, a sports star. Who didn't know his name? But Justin Braden isn't a star, is he? He's only famous because of his connection to Brett Falcone. No one outside the industry knows his name. Who the hell sits in a movie theater waiting to see who the writer was? No; I don't think this is going to help your boy's career."

Rob scowled. "I don't see you grieving losing a client," he pointed out.

Lou nodded. "It's a blow," he conceded. *Not as much for you as for Brett*, I thought; *talk about a poor word choice.* "But *Revenge* will clean up at the box office. There's a plaintive charm about dead movie stars. I don't mind working with his estate."

Brian, the personal assistant, said, "If you have the chance."

Lou considered him. "My role is spelled out in my contract," he said. "I'm perfectly clear about where I stand. If I were you, I'd check and see if you can say the same."

"Much as I hate interrupting this fascinating conversation," I said, "We're supposed to be figuring out who killed Brett. Everyone here seems to think it's not Justin, so it's up to us to come up with another option." And, I realized, I could very well be talking about someone in the room. "The question you're not asking is why. Why someone would want both Brett and Caroline dead." Part of me was afraid she was getting lost here, her murder eclipsed in the wake of the gossip and conjecture around Brett's.

"There's no motive that covers both of them," Austin said dismissively. "That's ridiculous. Maybe it's not the same person."

Seriously? This was one of Hollywood's great minds, and that was the best he could come up with?

Okay; I'd had enough. There's something about the film society that rubs me the wrong way, and these people were showing it in spades. The thing is, it's called the Provincetown International Film Festival, and the film society does get some work done that no one else is doing—a weekend of Jamaican films, for example, some other really creative endeavors—but only a few people on the board live in town, and there's always the impression they all see themselves as missionaries, bringing culture with a capital C to the locals.

But Brett and Caroline had both been killed here. The place had to count for something. It wasn't the only time they'd ever been together; had the killer not had access to them before? Or was it something that happened here and the killer had to step in? What about the movie? Was there something about *Revenge* that was dangerous? Brian said Brett was stepping out on Justin, and the movie title was a little too glaringly obvious.

And then the worst thought of all hit. I hadn't gotten Brett's autograph for my mother.

8

Where do you start? Motive? Modus operandi? For someone who was getting a reputation as the go-to person for murders in Provincetown, I knew woefully little about solving them.

Maybe I should take a course. There has to be a *PI for Dummies* book out there, something on YouTube maybe...

I left the whole flock of them arguing and headed out to my office-cum-cubbyhole. The kid at the front desk flashed me a smile. "Hey, Sydney? Can you tell me what I'm supposed to do with this? Mike isn't around and I don't know where he wants it."

"It" was a sleek MacBook. "Whose is it?" The front desk uses a complicated point-of-sale tablet for most transactions.

"It's that guy they arrested. Justin Braden."

I stared at him. "Why is it here?" And why didn't the police have it?

He was holding it slightly away from his body as if it were poisonous. "He was typing in it out by the pool yesterday," he said. "They argued about it. He kept saying he had a deadline, and Mr. Falcone told him to get his priorities straight. That was before they went to the awards ceremony. Mr. Braden said he didn't feel like going up to his room, so he asked me to hold it."

Sometimes you just get lucky. I grabbed the laptop with the alacrity of Ibsen when I offer him a treat and took off. My space is too public; I took the MacBook and retired to the restaurant, closed at this time of day. Sat at the empty bar. Took a deep breath. Yes, I was about to invade someone's privacy. But it was all in a good cause: clearing Justin, finding Brett's killer.

Now came the hard part: cracking the access password. I started thinking of possible combinations. His birthday. Brett's birthday. Did they have a dog? A lot of people used their pet's name. I'm one of them. This, I thought, was going to be challenging. This was going to be—

Justin didn't use a password.

The screen lit up with a photograph of Brett and Justin laughing together. I was in.

He used Apple Mail, the same as me, and I automatically clicked the stamp in the dock; it's the first thing I do when I boot up my computer and I wasn't even thinking when I did it to his. I had no plan. Anything was going to be fair game, here.

The emails were much like mine: the inbox was filled with subscriptions, offers, a plethora of names. He had separate mailboxes for Brett, for Rob Francis, for some other names I didn't recognize.

For Caroline Cooper.

I took a deep breath as a twinge of guilt hit. No, I told myself: I wasn't exactly snooping. Well, I was, but it was for the best of possible reasons. Still, there's something about reading someone else's emails…

"To hell with it," I said aloud, and clicked on the mailbox.

Nearly all the emails were professional: Caroline was producing the next movie, the one whose deadline Justin was up against. She was reminding him of what he'd told me at the party: that he was falling behind, she needed the script, there was a question of finances drying up. *I know you care about this project as much as I do,* Caroline had written. She sounded a little plaintive. *You've never been late before.*

It's all this stuff with Brett, wrote Justin.

It's always all this stuff with Brett. You have a career, too.

Not sure he sees it that way. Justin being wry.

Neither of them was explicit about what "the stuff" was; they both knew what they were talking about.

An hour later I was none the wiser about how to help Justin, though I did have a pretty good handle on what producers and screenwriters do, which was illuminating if probably irrelevant. The producer, I learned from Caroline's correspondence, is the central player in any film; she's the group leader and is responsible for managing the production from start to finish. She develops the project from the initial idea, makes sure the script is finalized, arranges the financing, and manages the production team that makes the film. She also coordinates the filmmaking process to ensure everyone involved in the project is working on schedule and on budget. Without the producer at the helm, films do not get made.

It all made me think there must be a wide swath of people who might have issues with a producer.

What was really interesting in all of this was that Caroline Cooper and Austin Hyde had co-produced *Revenge*. They were apparently not co-producers on whatever current project Justin was working on; but he'd been the *Revenge* screenwriter, too, so he'd worked as much with Austin as with Caroline, at least until filming wrapped some months ago. So why wasn't there a separate email inbox for Austin?

I was beginning to get a definite feeling about Mike's ex.

Sighing, I left the email program and looked for the current project; there might be a clue in what he was writing. Maybe someone didn't want their story told and bumping off Caroline was the way to do that. Maybe Brett was slated to play the lead—or maybe he wasn't, and that was the problem. Maybe Austin wanted to step into Caroline's position in the new project and Brett had seen him arguing with her. Maybe, maybe, maybe…

It didn't help that I didn't know the name of the film, or how Justin would refer to it or where he might file it. Probably not in a folder labeled *Project That Might Get Us All Killed*.

My phone beeped as a text came in. I pulled it out and looked: Mirela. *I am safely home here in Plovdiv*, she'd written.

Not sure how to respond—and with some guilt because, of course, I hadn't given her much thought at all since she'd left, though I did have an excellent excuse for that—I texted, *Glad to know*. After a moment, I added a smiley emoji.

My sister is well, but the baby is due quickly. I will tell you when it is born, and what I decide, she texted back.

Okay. Be careful. Careful? Of what? Did Bulgaria have werewolves or bigfoots? No; the danger to Mirela, I thought, was a great deal more subtle—and more treacherous. The call of family, of obligation, of ties that went back centuries and coursed through her blood. I sighed. How do you fight something like that?

I couldn't imagine Provincetown without Mirela. I couldn't imagine my life without Mirela. And it would surely break Ali's heart.

Thus reminded, I texted him, too. *Did you get to see Justin? Is he okay?*

A moment later the reply came back. *Not good. Doesn't care what happens to him. Can't get him to stop talking about Brett.*

I knew from Margo, my attorney friend, that keeping clients quiet was a big part of the job. People think the police are their friends. They're not. Justin was going to babble himself into a conviction if he wasn't careful.

I think the police should interview Austin Hyde, I typed.

Why?

Because I don't like him? *The movie will be a blockbuster now Brett's dead. Like a movie martyr. Austin stands to gain from that.*

So does everyone who gets a cut from the profits.

There's that, I thought, and sighed. Instead of having no suspects, it seemed we had a whole plethora of them to choose from. Who *didn't* benefit from Brett's death? *How long will you be there?*

For a while yet. His attorney just got here.

They'd made good time from Boston, those high-powered attorneys the LA contingent had called in. Probably flew in to the airport. On a private jet. *Okay, see you later,* I texted. I didn't mention I was reading Justin's emails; I somehow thought Ali wouldn't think it was such a very good idea.

Thus reminded, I turned back to the laptop. What had been going on between Brett and Justin that was fouling up Justin's attempts to get his work done? It couldn't be just common or garden-variety writer's block. I gathered it was unusual for him to be late with an assignment. I also gathered Caroline was none too sympathetic about whatever the issue was. Brett and Justin, the golden boys, their relationship shot through with something murky and deep and mysterious, something Justin had to apologize for, something indicating life wasn't quite as idyllic as it had seemed. What was "all this stuff with Brett"?

And did it have anything to do with his murder?

One of the kids who waited tables came into the room with an armful of flowers, ready to trim and place neatly in vases on each of the restaurant tables. He jumped visibly when he saw me. "Oh! Sorry, didn't think anyone was in here."

"It's fine," I said. "Just looking for a little peace and quiet."

"Oh. Is it okay if—?"

I motioned him to come in. "Go ahead, do what you have to do."

He came past me and spread the flowers out on the bar. I watched him, still toying with whatever was going on between Brett and Justin. Whatever it was, Julie was sure to be interested. Not that it was her case, with the Staties investigating; but if I knew Julie, she wasn't going to be deterred from trying to solve it, too. And she was laser-focused on Justin.

What I needed was a plausible alternative. What was it they said in court—reasonable doubt? Another option to consider. Austin.

I was watching the kid cutting flower stems without thinking about what I was seeing when something fired in my brain and made a connection. Back in the office, Lou speaking to Brian, Brett's snotty personal assistant. *I'm perfectly clear about where I stand. If I were you, I'd check and see I you can say the same.* And talking about Brett's will, the disposition of his finances. *There will be enough to afford flowers for the funeral, don't worry about that.*

Lou wasn't worried about the will, either the old one or the new one that now would never exist; people don't generally leave their estates to their agents. He's been trying to piss Rob off, and it had been working. He'd probably been the kind of kid who pulled wings off flies.

Lou probably didn't want Brett dead; but Caroline Cooper could be another story. After all, she was the one he'd negotiated contracts with. And there were more than enough producers to go around. He could even be in it with Austin.

I very much wanted it to be Austin.

***

I spent another hour with the MacBook and didn't get any further, and at some point someone was going to remember it had been left at the front desk; I couldn't hang onto it indefinitely. I found some porn, a surprising amount of really outstanding photography, folders filled with cocktail recipes, and a lot of screenplays, some with names I recognized, some half-finished and abandoned. Going by the dates the files were saved, it seemed that Justin had had a couple of projects underway at the same time. I didn't know anything about writing, but that seemed a little counterproductive. Maybe his problem *was* writer's block, after all.

I thought for a few minutes and then keyed Julie Agassi's contact icon on my phone.

She answered on the first ring. "Riley, do not, but do *not* tell me you have another body."

"And here I was going to be all helpful," I complained.

"Helpful is good."

"Okay. You'll thank me for this. I have Justin Braden's laptop computer."

There was a pause. "And you think this will help me how, exactly?"

I frowned. This conversation wasn't going in the direction I'd hoped. "Silly me," I said. "I thought you'd be delighted."

"Justin Braden was just released on bail," said Julie dispassionately. "I think he'll probably expect to find his computer untouched when he gets back to the inn. And in any case, no one's going to look at its contents without a warrant."

"Ah," I said. If Justin had been released, then both he and Ali might be showing up at any moment. This was a good thing.

"What does *ah* mean?" demanded Julie. "Riley, you haven't—"

"Gotta run," I interrupted cheerfully and disconnected. Well, I didn't have a warrant, did I? It would hardly do to say that to the head of detectives.

Twenty minutes later the front door opened and Ali and Justin and a serious guy in a suit came in. Suits really get noticed in Provincetown; unless you're getting married, you're probably not wearing one. The locals all dress casually and visitors all dress for vacation. This, I cleverly deduced, would be the attorney. Ali and Justin looked exhausted; the guy in the suit just looked like a guy in a suit.

Ali spotted me right away and came over. "It's ridiculous," he said, leaning his shoulder against the reception desk. His beautiful honey skin seemed gray.

"You look tired."

He shook his head. "Not as tired as he is," he said.

Justin and the attorney sat down in one of the lobby armchair arrangements, deep in conversation. "Listen, Ali, I've been thinking—" I began.

Ali held up his hand. "No," he said. "You're not investigating."

"I never realized how much you and Julie act alike," I said. "Mock me if you will, but there are some decent suspects right here in the inn as we speak." I broke off as a guest approached the desk, and I recognized Jack Donnelly, the film critic. "Hi, Sandy," he said.

"Sydney," I corrected.

"Sydney, right, sorry." He bestowed a bright smile on both of us. "Am I right in thinking that's Justin Braden over there?"

I turned to Ali. "Don't tell him anything," I said. "He's press."

"I'm a film critic," Jack corrected. He stuck out his hand to Ali. "Jack Donnelly. *Entertainment Weekly*. Don't worry, I don't do investigative journalism, anything like that. Review movies. Just curious, is all, you know?"

Ali shook his hand reluctantly. "Ali Hakim," he said.

The name didn't tell Jack anything, so he went back to the other topic. "I heard he was arrested," he said.

I wasn't impressed with his protestations of innocence: Jack was press, whatever else he might say, and if he got a juicy exclusive story he'd sell it in a heartbeat. "Apparently not," I said. "Seeing as he's here."

"Well, good then," Jack said and nodded vigorously. He slapped the top of the reception desk. "Well, gotta go! I've got two films to see and write up this afternoon. No rest for the wicked!"

Ali watched him go. "Are they all like that?" he asked.

"Who, reporters?"

"Buffoons," he said.

9

I had a cocktail party—*another* cocktail party—to at least look in on, back by the tiki bar and pool. The inn's constructed somewhat like the old Persian homes, with the building surrounding an open area of pool, bar, and events space where we did our weddings, complete with bower, café tables and chairs, all that jazz.

Ali came back with me and sat at the bar, drinking his usual tipple of ginger ale (sometimes, when he was feeling wild and crazy, he'd order orange juice) and chatting with the bartender. It was another of the film festival parties, where everyone squealed when they saw Someone Important and averted their eyes from anyone more lowly.

To absolutely no one's surprise, most of my usual suspects from the meeting in Glenn's office were there; these parties were important, the gossip they generated would ebb and flow through the movie community until the next film festival. We even had a wall set up at the end of the patio beyond the bower with a red carpet in front, and people standing in line to be photographed there.

I did my mingling is-everything-all-right, can-I-get-you-anything act for a few minutes. But the bartender was top-notch and the food being served by the handsome young men was some of Adrienne the diva chef's best; everyone seemed happy enough.

"So give me the cast of characters," said Ali when I joined him at the bar. I turned and leaned against it, shielding my eyes against the sun slanting in past the trees Barry had planted years ago around the patio.

"Okay," I said. "So that kid over there, the one scarfing Adrienne's *vol au vent?* That's Brian Somebody. He was Brett's personal assistant. Very full of himself and his importance in the great scheme of things. Not sure who he's going to ingratiate himself with next."

"Young Brian didn't exactly appeal to you," Ali observed.

"You could say that," I agreed. "Moving along. Standing oh-so-temptingly by the pool is Rob Francis."

"Ah," said Ali, nodding. "I heard a lot about him today. Justin's agent."

"That's right. What did you hear?"

"Justin's thinking of *going in another direction,*" said Ali, putting air-quotes around the expression. "But he's contractually committed to at least another year with Francis, and it isn't making him happy. He thinks Rob's skimming. Had an accountant look at the books a couple months ago. He thought he'd get through the wedding, see his folks in Boston, get back home and talk to a lawyer."

"Not, presumably, the same one he's talking to now."

"Different issue," said Ali. "This one's criminal."

"Aren't they all?" I asked lightly. Sometimes I just can't help myself. "Okay. Moving along. Mike, of course, you know." I was looking at the people around the pool. I had a private bet with myself that at some point at least one of them was going to end up in it. "He's talking to a blonde woman I don't know, but the kind of portly guy with the cigar, he's Lou Estrada, and he's Brett's agent. Or was, anyway." For all I knew, Lou might go on representing Brett's estate in perpetuity.

"No one," said Ali thoughtfully, "seems overcome with grief."

"Even Justin?" I asked. "How is he taking all this?"

He blew out a long breath. "He's devastated. I'm glad I went right down there, he wasn't in good shape and the guy from the state police had every intention of taking advantage of it." He shrugged, quickly. "What I'd do in his place," he admitted. "I don't think it's sunk in that he's a person of interest. All he wants to do is be alone and deal with— whatever it is he's feeling. I can't pretend to know that." He took a quick swallow of ginger ale. "I think he's safe for now. They're good cops, those guys, they're not fixating on just the one lead."

"Nice of you to offer them professional courtesy," I said, gesturing to the bartender. "Can I get a glass of red wine, please?"

"I'm just saying what I saw. I was impressed," Ali said. "He's calling his sister to come stay with him. He has to stay here for now, and he doesn't want to be alone."

I took the wineglass from the bartender and turned to survey the party again. "Not

with that bunch of hyenas, for sure," I said.
"She lives in Boston? The sister?"

"Yeah, how'd you know?"

"He told me his family's there. He went to
BU."

"Well, she's on her way now. Taking the
ferry. I said we'd meet her, hope that's okay.
If you're busy I can go alone."

I took a sip of wine. Ah; things looked bet-
ter already. "Of course I'll go with you," I said.
"And I'll arrange for a room for her, too.
What's the name?"

"Eleanor. Ellie for short."

"Okay." Another sip of wine. "And of
course I haven't yet shown you the prince of
princes, the co-producer whose producing
partner got killed, and the man whose effigy I
plan to stick pins in," I said. "That would be
Austin Hyde, over there in the unfortunate
tie."

Ali raised his eyebrows. "Not just the tie
that's unfortunate," he said. "Is that a soul
patch?" I took a deep breath and he put a restraining hand on my arm. "You are *not* singing Smashmouth," he said.

"How did you know I was about to?"

"Sheer brilliance. You know my ways, Watson. You've been humming it since yesterday."

I hate it when I'm obvious. "So now you have the cast of characters," I said.

"The question is, did any of them have a motive?"

I considered the options. "For Caroline Cooper or Brett Falcone?"

"You can't think they're not connected."

I sighed. "No," I agreed. "It's stretching coincidence too far if they're not. So... I wouldn't be surprised if Austin and Caroline were up against myriad issues. Co-producing a movie means two cooks in the kitchen instead of one."

"And *Revenge* had a lot of problems," said Ali.

"Really?" I turned to him. "I haven't heard about that. Like what?"

"Over on schedule. *Way* over on budget. The leading lady was hell on wheels to work with and was driving the production team to distraction. She and Brett hated each other and the romantic scenes were a disaster, they had to keep shooting them over and over. Even Justin wasn't helping—he kept turning in new rewrites, he was having problems getting it done."

"I know," I said, then drew in my breath sharply, remembering that I wasn't supposed to know that.

Ali didn't seem to notice. "The director quit," he said. "Apparently your friend Austin was riding him pretty hard and he saw the writing on the wall."

"For a couple of mixed metaphors," I observed.

Ali laughed. "It's hanging out with Justin that does it," he said, massaging his chin. "Man, this guy's supposed to be all that in the screenwriting world, but honestly, Sydney, for a writer, he thinks in breathtakingly bad clichés. Maybe his bad habits rubbed off on me. Anyway, the long and short of it is, they didn't think they were even going to get the film editing finished in time for Provincetown, and Brett was going ballistic over it, he really wanted it here, and he knew the film society was giving him the award, so he got crazy when it looked like it wasn't happening. Justin says he kept screaming at people about how he was going to get an award when he didn't even have a film in the can. He was screaming at Justin about the rewrites, too. Said Justin kept losing his—Brett's, that is—voice."

"I'm starting to think this would have been easier if it had been Justin who was killed," I said.

Ali stared at me. "Say that again."

"What?" I took a sip of wine. "Sounds like Justin was underperforming and getting on everyone's last nerve. Based on that, maybe he should've been the one murdered, not Brett. Brett was just throwing temper tantrums, which seems to be par for the course with these boys." I narrowed my eyes. "Why? What are you thinking?"

"Probably nothing," he said and shrugged. "But from everything I see, there'd be enough motives with this bunch for any of them to be killed."

"You got that right." I looked at my watch. "Time for the ferry."

But I wondered, even as I finished off my wine and we left for MacMillan Pier, what it was I'd said that brought that gleam of interest to Ali's eyes.

I hoped it was something good. Because I was batting zero as a crime-solver at the moment.

***

Ellie Braden looked just like a female version of Justin; she'd added in a lot of dark curls cascading down her back and a curvy figure, but the essentials were the same, the wide blue eyes, the even white teeth. She was struggling a little with her roller-wheels and I poked Ali in the ribs. "Time for you to go and rescue the damsel in distress," I said.

I watched him greet her and extricate the bag from the curb it had hooked itself onto. I learned early in our relationship to trust him. Ali's gorgeous—I may have mentioned this already—and every straight woman and every gay man in a ten-mile radius finds him attractive. He and Mirela have a very close friendship, and Mirela's no slouch in the looks department, either. I figured very early on with Ali I could spend all my time fretting about people coming on to him, or trust him when he told me he loved me. I'd opted for the latter.

"Sydney, this is Ellie."

She was breathless and pretty, in a fifties-style dress of red polka dots, cinched in tight at the waist with a red patent-leather belt. "I didn't know what to pack," she was saying.

"Oh, hi, I'm sorry, gosh, you must think I'm so rude. I'm Ellie Braden." She stuck out her hand and I took it. "Sydney Riley," I said.

"It's so kind of you to meet me. I feel a little lost." She'd turned the blue eyes and the dark eyelashes back to Ali, and, I *swear*, batted them at him.

He looked amused. "We'll get you to the inn," he said. "Your brother is anxious to see you."

She looked from him to me. "Tell me the truth," she said. "Is he really in trouble?"

"We hope not," said Ali, taking the lead with the suitcase. "Let's go."

I said to Ellie, "I'm so sorry for your loss. For Brett."

"Yes," she said, and the wide blue eyes filled with tears. Almost on cue, I thought, and found myself wondering, fleetingly, if Justin's sister might not be an actor herself. Or maybe I was looking for mysteries where there were none. She tossed her curls over her shoulder. "And it's especially sad, you know, since we were looking so forward to seeing them both. Um, after the wedding, and all that."

And yet, I thought, *you weren't actually invited to the ceremony*. Something a little off, there. Wedding guests come to Provincetown from a lot farther away than Boston. Why hadn't Justin's family been invited? Now that I thought about it, neither groom had had any family there. It had to have been deliberate.

I resolved to mention it to Ali.

Ellie managed, bravely, to just about keep up with us in her high heels. I tried at first to make some small talk, but it was really impossible with the volume of people on Commercial Street; we had to keep ducking and weaving through pedestrian traffic and stay the hell out of the way of whizzing bicycles. About a third of the people we saw were wearing film festival lanyards and tags.

At the inn, she sank down immediately into one of the velvet armchairs by the front desk and rubbed an ankle. "I didn't really dress for a long walk," she said ruefully with a smile that may have been meant to take the sting out of her words but instead made it pointedly clear that a taxi would have been a far better option.

I wondered if perhaps Justin had been adopted. Appearances aside, this woman wasn't much like him, or at least the way he'd been during the times we were together. Justin was the one who went for refills of drinks; Ellie was used to being waited on. Apparently

157

there wasn't much chance of her checking herself in, anyway. I grabbed the tablet computer from the front desk and stood awkwardly in front of her, getting her information down, holding the tablet for her to sign. Ali had disappeared, the coward.

Mike ambled by and paused. "No one working the desk?" he asked pleasantly. I knew him well enough to detect the shadow of menace behind the pleasantness; I pitied the poor person who'd stepped away for five minutes.

"I've got it," I said cheerfully. "Mike, this is Ellie Braden, Justin's sister. Ellie, this is Mike, the Race Point Inn's manager."

He went from menacing to sunny in one second flat. "Ms. Braden. Welcome. I am so sorry for your loss. I know your brother will be pleased to see you."

"And no news," said Ellie, holding onto his hand and looking seductively up at him through the thick lashes, "on what really happened to poor Brett?"

Mike glanced at me while trying to extricate his hand from her grip. He was leaning uncomfortably over her and she must have known what she was doing. "The police are investigating," he said. "Sydney actually knows more about it than I do."

Thanks a lot, I mouthed to him over her head. "I know they're following several leads," I said, loudly and cheerfully. "Here's your key-card, you're in eighteen, which is in the back of the building. I'll take you there, if you'd like."

She had to let go of Mike to take the card, and he straightened up hastily. "Thank you, Sydney," she said primly, and waited a moment. When neither of us made a move to assist her out of the chair, she gathered her courage and managed to propel her own little self to her feet. "I must look a sight! All that wind on the ferry!"

"We can go up now," I said grimly. "And then I'm sure you want to see Justin." We'd moved Justin from the suite he'd shared with Brett—the police weren't finished there anyway—to a more private room in another part of the inn. The press was already sniffing around, and not just film reviewers like Jack and Irene, either. The inn had to do everything possible to safeguard his privacy.

"Yes, of course, poor Justin!" she exclaimed, then turned to Mike. "Thank you for everything. I'll see you again soon, won't I?"

Mike looked a little wildly at me. "Of course," he said to Ellie. He seemed totally befuddled. Women didn't usually flirt with him, especially not a woman who looked like she'd stepped off the set of *Mad Men*. Or *I Love Lucy*.

Lucy was probably, sad to say, more *my* cup of tea. I managed to get Ellie up a flight of stairs without her expiring on the way, though to hear her sighs it was a close thing. I was wondering just how much contact I was going to have to have with Justin's sister when a group of people emerged from one of the suites across the hall, and timing is everything, isn't it, because they were the last people I wanted to see—and that I wanted to see Ellie.

Rob, Austin, Lou, Brian, a couple of guys I didn't know, all deep in discussion. All the boys in the band. Of course the damned keycard didn't work the first five times. That's always what happens when you're in a hurry, isn't it?

Ellie was already giving them what I was coming to think of as her patented smile. She *had* to be in the business herself, I thought: it's the same smile I'd been seeing all over town already. Rob stopped when he saw her. "Eleanor," he said, not looking any too pleased about it.

"Hello, Rob." Ellie gave him a lower kilo-watt version of the smile. "So nice to see you, also, but so sad, too, isn't it?"

The others hadn't waited; they were drifting down the hallway, still deep in discussion. Rob glanced after them and then back to Ellie. "We'll have a chance to talk later," he said to her.

The smile widened. "I'm looking forward to it."

I'd finally managed to make the electronic lock work, and was holding the door open. "Here you go, Ellie, this is you."

"I'll see you later, Rob," she said brightly and turned to me. "Thank you, Cindy."

"Sydney." No one seemed to be able to get my name right. What was it about these film people? Did they even *listen* to names?

Ellie walked past me and inspected the room. It was small and cozy, which pretty much describes every room in Provincetown. Including my apartment. "Where is my brother, do you know?"

I shook my head. "I'll find out. Why don't you relax a few minutes, unpack, and then come downstairs?"

"All right." She sounded like she was pouting. She sat down on the bed, bounced up and down a couple of times. I left her to it.

It was actually a good thing, I thought once I was alone in the corridor, that we'd run into Rob and he'd recognized Ellie. I'd been starting to think that she might not be Justin's sister at all.

Ali was sitting at the bar drinking ginger ale when I got downstairs. "Was she what you expected?"

"Not even close." I climbed onto the stool next to him and signaled the bartender. "Same as him." It was late afternoon, some of the films were letting out, people were drifting in for an aperitif. Soon the inn would be full. It should have been a relaxing time. "Ali, why do you think she wasn't invited to the wedding?"

"Ah. I wondered when you were going to catch that," he said.

"It doesn't make sense. *You* live in Boston, and you're down here all the time."

"Don't remind me, *cara*." It was a conversation we kept tabling, the question of when and how and whether we could live together. To be honest, Ali was doing the heavy lifting when it came to commuting; he was, consequently, the one who brought the question up more frequently.

I glossed over it, as I always did. "She got here in record time, since you only called her, what? This morning? And the wedding's been planned for eons. No one could say the family was taken by surprise."

"One might detect," said Ali, "some family turmoil there. Maybe Justin's estranged from them."

"He sounded fine when he was talking about them at the cocktail party," I objected. "Said that they knew Brett, of course, but that he and Brett still had to visit. I think he said something about showing off the wedding rings, maybe getting a wedding present." Not for the first time, I wished I hadn't had quite so much champagne at that party. "I didn't pick up on anything that overwhelmingly negative." That kind of anger, I thought, would surely have penetrated even my alcohol-induced haziness, would have been blazingly obvious.

"And that doesn't strike you as odd?" asked Ali. "They have to go up to show off their rings to the very people they snubbed by not inviting them to the wedding? And, what, get presents from them? Something's going on there. Something's not right."

"Possible," I acknowledged, and sipped my own ginger ale. "But the question is, whatever it is, does it have anything to do with Brett or Caroline's deaths?"

He nodded. "That *is* the question," he agreed.

We were saved from any more musings by the appearance of Ellie herself, looking fresh and ready for more flirting. At least she'd exchanged her high heels for red flats; the girl was learning. "Cocktails! I love cocktails!" she exclaimed, and turned the high-wattage smile on the bartender. "Oh, something exotic, don't you think?"

I was staring at her. Her brother-in-law murdered, her brother a suspect in the crime, and she was in a celebratory mood? Ali and I exchanged glances. "Justin will be down in a few minutes," Ali told her.

"Good. He can have a cocktail, too!" She pondered a moment before ordering a Manhattan, sticking seamlessly with the *Mad Men* theme she had going.

I was starting to wonder if she might actually be mentally deficient when she turned to me. "I have to tell you, I'm not actually a bitch, Sydney," she said.

I swallowed. "Ellie. I never—"

She waved it away. "It's okay. I know you were thinking it, even if you were too polite to say. The thing is, you just have to know, there's a lot no one's told you. Some things aren't what they look like." She smiled again for the bartender, who'd put her drink in front of her. She raised it in the air. "To poor dead Brett," she said.

Ali and I were both staring at her. Neither of us lifted a glass.

Ellie drank half the glass in one swallow and put it down with a thump. "Okay," she said. "Here's the thing. Justin's a dear, and all, and everybody adores him, or would, except that no one does, not really, because first of all, it has to be taken as a given: men in our family just aren't gay."

It was an old story, heartbreaking every time it became new again. "So what happened? Did your parents disown him, or something?"

She shook her head; the curls bounced. "No, of course not, nothing that overt," she said. "We had to keep up appearances. We live in Back Bay. Do you know Boston?" She didn't wait for an answer. "It's very exclusive, where we live. The brownstone's been in our father's family for generations and generations. People have expectations of us. Mother's on the board of the Museum of Fine Arts. There's a wing of Mass. General named after our grandfather. So that's what I'm trying to tell you. As long as Justin kept it to himself, everything was fine."

Everything was not fine, I diagnosed, not even a little bit. For Justin. Maybe also for the little sister forced to be as girly a girl as she could by way of compensation.

Ellie had taken advantage of the pause for another hefty swallow of her Manhattan and finished it off. I'd never seen anyone drink that much, that fast. "And then Justin went off to school and you know how it is, when they don't see what's happening, they can pretend it isn't there. And we could have gone on like that for a long time, really we could have. But then a couple of things happened."

Ali said, "Here's Justin now."

Timing is, as they say, everything.

10

Ellie turned her brightest-ever smile on her brother. "Justin!" She turned away from the bar and put her arms around him. He was looking at us over her shoulder, almost wooden by comparison. "Come have a drink, darling. You don't look good."

"No," said Justin, "I don't suppose I do."

More people were trickling into the room, ready for drinks, some of them already considering food so they could get out and catch some evening films. The festival movies were in venues all over town, all the time; it was a labyrinth, trying to weave one's way from one to another, both in time and in geography.

The bar was filling, and Ali pulled a stool over for Justin. "Here you go."

"Thanks." He looked exhausted.

Ellie got the bartender's attention with a blink of the lashes. "He'll have what I'm having," she said. "And I'll have another one, too."

Nothing passed over Justin's face when she ordered for him.

There was a lull while we waited. Ali was casually watching the room, his cop's eyes not missing anything. Down at the other end of the bar I saw Irene and Jack, the film critics. Glenn had assigned one of the staff to keep reporters off the premises, but I supposed that, as they were guests at the inn, the rule didn't apply to them. Somewhere behind me I could hear Austin's very recognizable reedy voice raised in a petulant whine.

The cocktails arrived. "Drink that," Ellie ordered. "You'll feel better."

"Justin," said Ali, "we're trying to help, if we can. Sydney's—well, she's pretty good at this kind of thing." I gave him a look: *pretty good?* We'd have words about that later. Then again, I wasn't even living up to lukewarm praise, not right at that moment. "She can help. But we have to figure out who did this, so they'll leave you alone." He was speaking slowly and patiently, his speech at about the right level, I thought, for Justin's current capacity to comprehend what was going on.

He'd taken a swallow and put the glass down. "I didn't kill Caroline," he said.

"We know," said Ali.

"And I didn't kill Brett."

"We know," I said. "But we have to prove that."

Ellie said, smiling brightly, "We were talking about the family."

He raised his eyes from the glass to his sister's face. "Do they know? Mom and Dad, do they know?"

She patted his hand. "Of course they know, silly! And it's all going to turn out fine, you'll see. You're still invited to come and stay with us when all this"—a gesture that encompassed the restaurant and possibly even the world at large—"is over."

"Good. Okay." He nodded as if satisfied. "It'll be fine if—"

He was interrupted by the arrival of two men, Staties in plain clothes if I'd ever seen them. I'd met a few, but didn't know either of these guys. "Justin Braden? We'd appreciate it if you'd come with us."

Ali slid off his stool. He clearly *did* know them. "Really? He just got back from spending time with you," he said crisply.

"Agent Hakim, please step aside."

"Why do you want him?" Ali turned to Justin without waiting for an answer. "Call your lawyer. *Now*," he said. Justin fumbled with his phone, looking dazed. As well he might: it seemed the police station was equipped with a revolving door.

"We've received additional information," said the taller of the two detectives.

"Is Mr. Braden under arrest?" Ali can sound as authoritarian as anyone, any day of the week.

"Not at this time. Just a few friendly questions."

"If it's that friendly," I said. "Then why not do it here?"

Justin had reached his guy on the phone. I realized I could hear him clearly because the noise around us had died down. Everybody was staring. There was a sudden sound of clattering as someone dropped dishes in the kitchen; I saw, out of the corner of my eye, Martin moving in that direction.

"It's all right," Justin said dully. "I'll go with them." I could almost sense the wave of disappointment washing over the room: they were to be deprived of still more delicious drama, far more fun than anything they were seeing on the silver screen.

"I think that's a good idea," said one of the Staties.

They waited until Justin had another gulp of his drink and slid off the stool. "Clarence is meeting me there again," he said to Ali.

"Good. Anything else you need?"

He shook his head, then jerked it toward Ellie. "Keep an eye on her for me?" he asked.

Ali nodded. I grabbed the moment to address one of the Staties. "You said you received additional information. What is it? From whom did you receive it?"

"That information's only available on a need-to-know basis," he said.

"I'd say we need to know," I snapped. "You're disrupting dinner service, dragging this man out in the most public display of—" I stopped with Ali's hand on my arm. "Leave it," he said quietly.

"I will not! They have to tell us. They're supposed to be transparent in what they do," I said. I had no idea whether or not that was true.

Ali said, "I'll go with him. I'll find out. *Cara*, you have to take care of Ellie."

They were already out the door when I realized that for sure I'd just drawn the short straw. "Well," said Ellie brightly, "I guess that means it's time for another drink!" She signaled the bartender. I thanked my lucky stars I was guzzling ginger ale rather than wine, my normative first choice.

I waited until she was well into her third Manhattan. "So you were going to tell me. What is the family problem?" I asked.

She was starting to seem a little fuzzy. "Which one? 'Cause, you know, we've got more'n one. Big family, big problems." She found that hilarious and I had to wait for her to stop laughing.

"What do you think the police found out, that they want to question Justin about now?" I asked.

"Could be anything. Can I get another one of these?" She wasn't looking at me or the drink, but off toward the end of the bar. Who knows what shiny thing had caught her increasingly drunken attention. "I really, really need another one of those," she said, with slightly more force, and I saw that her hand was trembling.

I gestured no to the bartender, shaking my head. "I think you've probably had enough." I couldn't get a handle on what was happening: was this her normal reaction to stress, or was tonight something special? "I think we should get you something to eat," I said.

"Not hungry," she mumbled. "Gotta go. Better find ladies' room before he sees me." She slid off her stool, bounced up against me, and slid to the floor, completely out of it.

My interrogation skills clearly left something to be desired.

***

Ali got home after ten, and was visibly irate. "Someone out there really wants Justin to go down for this," he said, sitting on the edge of the bed and taking off his shoes with somewhat more force than strictly necessary.

I'd been watching television, mostly for white noise—my rent's cheap because I live over a nightclub, and the dance floor was in full swing tonight. Not everybody was here for the film festival.

"That's stupid," I said. I wasn't going to attempt to get out of the sofa to go join him; it was way too much of a struggle. Maybe someday I'll own a sofa that doesn't try to swallow you whole. "Everyone knows the two murders are connected, and Justin couldn't have killed Caroline, he never left the restaurant."

"No one seems to be coming up with a credible alternative theory of it all," Ali said. "Damn, I'm tired. Is there anything to eat?"

It's worth noting: just because I own a refrigerator doesn't mean this was a ridiculous question. "I thought you were coming here this week to cook for me," I pointed out. "But there's some chicken salad in there." I thought for a moment. "I *think* it's still good."

He pulled his phone out. "I'm not taking the chance," he said, and called Julie Knapp at Twisted for pizza delivery.

I was hard at thought while he called. "You said someone's trying to set Justin up," I said. "And those guys tonight, they said they had new information. It had to come from somewhere. Who's doing that? Who's giving them new information?"

"Damned if I know," said Ali. "But you yourself said there's a plethora of suspects, and probably any one of them would be glad to see him take the fall."

"So what was this new information that had them dragging him back out there?"

"Anonymous tip," he said, disgust in his voice. "Emailed to Julie. And before you say it, no, it's not traceable. Anyone who's half-decent at hacking can spoof anything. It's not rocket science."

I started the process of extricating myself from the sofa. "And this mysterious email said…?"

"Justin's been left some money," Ali said. "It would be useful to talk to Ellie and see if she knows anything about it." We'd already had a conversation about Ellie, who was tucked in and snoring in her room at the inn. Mike had gotten one of his handsome young men to carry her up.

"*That's* not happening tonight," I said.

"I know. Tomorrow. Anyway, seems the family had a hard time with Justin being gay."

"Yeah, she mentioned that."

"And with Brett in particular. I mean, there was general rejection around the gay thing, but there was personalized rejection of Brett. Don't know why, but apparently there's some sort of convoluted trust so that if Justin either divorced Brett, or if Brett died, Justin was in for a windfall."

This was new. "What kind of windfall?"

"The kind," said Ali, "that gets people killed."

I'd finally staggered to my feet and started getting plates out for pizza. "Who would know that kind of thing?" I demanded. There was silence behind me. "What?" I said, turning around, my hands filled with cutlery. "*What?*"

"Who would know?" asked Ali rhetorically. "Justin, that's who."

"Oh, hell, this is ridiculous," I said. "Everyone's talking about money. You've got this trust thing. This morning, they were all talking about insurance money on Brett's death. And Justin's inheritance as his spouse."

"Everyone's talking about money because it's one of the major incentives for homicide," said Ali. "Time-tested and almost always true. Greed's a tremendous motivator. Why wouldn't we be talking about money?"

"Two reasons," I snapped. "Number one, Justin doesn't need any more money. He's rich in his own right, and he and Brett were going to be rich together. No, wait." I held up a hand to keep Ali from speaking. "Before you say anything, there's reason number two, and that's that they were crazy about each other. I've seen a million weddings." All right, so that's a *slight* exaggeration. "And I've never seen a couple like them. They were perfect. They were made for each other. They were meant to be together. He'd rather have Brett alive than any money, any day." I took a deep breath. "And I'd like to know who it is that's whispering these sweet nothings in the police's shell-like ears. Maybe *that's* someone we should be looking at!"

The doorbell rang. "And how do you propose to find out who it is?" Ali demanded. "Use your crystal ball?" He *was* tired; Ali's not usually sarcastic. He leaves that part of the relationship to me.

The doorbell rang again. "I'm not going downstairs," I said.

"Oh, for Pete's sake!" My foul-mouthed boyfriend. He grabbed his wallet and headed down the stairs in his socks.

I poured drinks, ginger ale for him and a Malbec for me. It was definitely time to temper my—well, *temper*—with some alcohol. By the time he was upstairs with the pizza I'd also managed to locate and light a couple of mismatched candles. No one can say I'm a slouch when it comes to being romantic.

I was still wondering who it was that knew so much about Justin's family finances. At least I knew who to ask.

11

Ellie Braden was definitely the worse for wear. She sat at the breakfast table in the inn's main dining room wearing sunglasses and a shapeless sweater, not quite the perky *Mad Men* girl-about-town of the previous day.

She looked at me without enthusiasm when I pulled up a chair at her table. "Feel free to yell at me," she said. "Except—don't yell."

"You do that sort of thing often?" I signaled the waiter for coffee.

"What? Find out my brother's going to jail for the rest of his life? No, not often."

Wow. And I thought *I* was able to jump from zero to the worst possible conclusion in a single bound. Ellie made me look like an amateur in the advanced anxiety free-throw.

My coffee arrived and I took that first sip. Lovely. "Okay," I said, putting down the cup. "We have to be honest with each other here, and you have to tell me what's going on. Did your father really say he'd only release Justin's trust if Brett wasn't in the picture anymore?"

She nodded. "Oh, it's silly, really, but he has it in his head that if Brett weren't around, Justin would go back to being—normal—again." Cool. Now the father could reasonably be in the frame, too. "He has it in his head that Brett's bad for Justin. It's stupid. Justin's not going to suddenly turn straight. And he's not moving back to Boston, with or without Brett. He doesn't even like *visiting*, he hates every minute of it."

"Why?"

She stared at the scrambled egg in front of her and pushed the plate aside. "What would really *help* would be a cigarette," she said irritably.

"Sorry. I don't smoke." And I'm not about to let you bum a cigarette and go outside to smoke it without answering my questions. "Why doesn't Justin like Boston? And why did your father blame Brett for everything?"

Ellie sighed. "Really. It's just so tedious. Justin didn't have a lot of friends there," she said. "He's a total introvert, you know. Writers are like that. Writers like being by themselves. It doesn't really matter where they live, you know, because they never leave their rooms." Interesting perspective, but I didn't have time to follow up on it. "Even when he was in college, Justin didn't do the party scene, he didn't hang out with anyone. He was probably hooking up with other gay men back then, I don't know anything about that, but he sure didn't have a lot of other people in his life. No friends that I ever met." She shrugged. "You have no idea, Cindy, he just couldn't *wait* to get out of town. And then when he got his first job in LA—well, that was when he met Brett, and *that* was the end of everything else for him. Brett was all he cared about. Brett, and his writing."

"But then, he could write from Boston," I pointed out. "Maybe he *will* come back, now that Brett's gone."

She shook her head. "You don't understand," she said. "It's the *city* he hates. He'll never do it. He says it's bad luck. The whole city, can you imagine? How can a city be bad luck? How does that work?" She shrugged; the question was rhetorical. "He's probably saying that right now, in fact. He's probably saying

181

it's because they planned to go to Boston that Brett got killed. Superstitious as hell. And of course one little thing happened, just this one thing, and he said it proved he was right. The only time he came back, he saw something, a crime, and that meant he had to come back again, another time, for the trial, and it really ate at him, that whole thing, the violence and the trial."

I nodded. "He told me about it," I said.

"Yeah? I'm not surprised. It seems to have really marked him. I don't understand why. It's not like he got hurt. It's not like anybody he knew got hurt. It was just one of those things." She stirred her coffee but didn't drink any. "Our mother's dying," she said, an echo of something different, something sad and sweet in her voice. "She has cancer. They stopped the treatments, they weren't working anyway and they were making her miserable. I think Father would do anything to get Justin back to spend time with her."

Wow. That opened up a whole new avenue of thought. But it couldn't be; even if Justin's father had taken out a hit on Brett—and how preposterous was that, honestly?— he'd have had no reason to kill Caroline. And her murder was different anyway...

I followed my own trailing thoughts. Wait. Maybe I was onto something. Wasn't that a problem? If my own experience and reading were anything to go by, killers stick to the same methods, the ones that are comfortable for them. Caroline Cooper was strangled; Brett Falcone had been struck by mystery's beloved blunt object. Could it be different people? Could it really have been a coincidence that they were both murdered in the same week, at the same place? Wasn't strangling a method favored by women, and whacking someone over the head favored by men?

I just couldn't see it.

"Who knows about all this?" I asked Ellie. "Because Justin getting picked up for questioning last night? That's because someone told the police about the trust fund." This was a pretty significant lead, I thought: someone really, really wanted Justin in custody. It hadn't taken them long: he'd been released yesterday, early afternoon, and by evening the police had received the tip about the money.

He was back in his room at the inn now; Mike told me he'd been released yet again. I wondered if his presence here meant something else, some other bit of "evidence," would be passed on to the police today.

It was almost as if Justin were the shiny object someone wanted us all to pay attention to. Magicians work that way: they get you to focus where they want you to, on one thing they toss up or hold in front of your face, so you don't notice what else they're doing on the side.

Ellie was shaking her head. "No one," she said. "No one knew. The fund's from our grandmother, we both have one, and Father has the purse strings. She gave the money, but he got to determine the conditions."

"What are your conditions?" I asked curiously. "I mean, what do *you* have to do to inherit?" It was none of my business, of course, and probably not even relevant to what was going on now, but I'm fascinated by the control some people exert over others. Especially through lucre.

Besides, I'm just plain nosy.

She tried her coffee and put it back down with a clatter, no doubt finding it cold. "I have to get married and have a baby," she said.

That was startling, in the twenty-first century, anyway. "Really? Um—do you have plans to? To do—what he wants you to do?"

"I'll have to, won't I?" Her voice was morose. "I don't have a lot of choices. I want to have pretty things and I want to go to Gstaad in the winter, and I'm not like Justin, you have to understand. I guess talent doesn't run in the family. I don't have any discernable forte, not like Justin. I'm not brilliant at anything. I can get by, but I won't in a million years be able to make that kind of money on my own. So I'll have to do it." She sighed. "It doesn't matter. I'll deal with it eventually, when I really need the inheritance. I'm living at home at the moment, I don't really need it yet. Right now it's just about getting through Mom's… stuff."

That did it for me. This family was bracing itself for a grief that would make the earth move on its axis, and I was suspecting the father of murder. I really ought to be ashamed.

Ellie put her elbows on the table and leaned into her hands. "God, I feel like shit."

Having been there myself, and quite recently, I didn't want to push her any further. "Have some more coffee," I suggested. "Maybe—"

She was looking past me and came out of her chair with more alacrity that I could manage on a good day. Then again, I had about ten years and ten pounds on her. "Justin!"

He was looking a little lost. His sister hugged him and led him—literally—back to our table. "Good morning," he said to me, and "thanks," as Ellie pulled out a chair and pushed him into it. For someone who played the helpless-female card to perfection, Ellie was also pretty damned good at taking charge. I wondered what that meant.

If Ellie had been looking the worse for wear, Justin looked like it was one-foot-in-the-grave time. "Are you all right?" I asked, then mentally kicked myself. Good one, Riley. Of course he's not all right.

He gave me a wan smile. "I just got off the phone," he said to no one in particular. "They're not releasing—Brett—until they've done an autopsy. I can't believe it. They already know how he died—what killed him."

I nodded. "It's the law," I said. I had a little experience here. "They've probably done it already, in fact. Right after you identified him."

"So why can't I—can't the funeral home—?" He shook his head in frustration. "It's hard enough already to get him shipped back home," he said. "All these things you never think about until they happen to you."

"I know," I said, putting as much comfort as I could into my voice. It had never occurred to me, either, that the body would be a problem. Are there coffins mixed in with the baggage on commercial flights? If a plane crashes, are there remains among the—remains?

And what was going to happen to Caroline? I didn't know anything about her. Was someone grieving her, now? Was someone waiting for her body to be released so it could be sent home? I pretty much had front-row seats to The Brett Murder Show, but knew nothing about Caroline Cooper. And if it were the same murderer...

Justin ordered coffee and I told the waiter to bring a plate of pastries as well. Partly because these two needed their blood sugar levels elevated, partly because I adore the work of Angus, our Scottish pastry chef. "What happens now?" I asked.

Justin looked at his watch. "I have to be at the cinema at Whaler's Wharf at eleven," he said. Seeing my look, he said, "We're giving a talk. Well, Brett was going to be there, too, and Caroline, but now it's just going to be me and Austin."

"Talking about what? Can't you cancel it?"

He shook his head. "Brett would have gone, if it was me who'd been killed," he said, which seemed an extraordinary statement, but, okay, whatever. "We were going to talk about our different roles. Me as screenwriter, Caroline as producer, Brett as actor. It's a perk for some of the big donors. It's important to do. And Austin said he'd stand in for Caroline. So I really do have to go."

It was five past ten. "Have something to eat first," I said, as the waiter put a platter on the table. I grabbed one and wrapped it in a napkin: pastry to go. I stood up. "I have to go do something," I said. "But I'll send a car for you at half past."

"We can walk," Justin protested, but I shook my head. "This is better. You'll have more privacy." Ellie and I exchanged a glance over his head, and she nodded. "Thank you," she said quietly.

Mike was talking to the kid at the front desk. "Sydney! Are we really still holding a room for this guy—what's his name?"

"George Tate," said the kid at the desk.

"George Tate? He's supposed to be here for something to do with the film festival, but didn't check in last night."

"I have no idea," I said. "Listen, can you get the car and have someone pick Justin and Ellie up at ten-thirty to go to Whaler's Wharf?"

"Okay," said Mike, automatically checking his watch. There was something going on there, I sensed, something not quite right with him. He was worried about something, something beyond the usual inn stuff and whether or not someone called George Tate had showed up. I wished he'd talk to me. "Ellie? That's the sister?"

I pushed my concern about Mike aside and nodded. "He's giving a talk at eleven."

He watched me head toward the door. "And where are you going?"

"I'll be there, too," I said. Because the one thing that connected Caroline and Brett and Justin and Austin was Whaler's Wharf.

It was time to find out why.

***

It was, I had to admit, a remarkably pleasant day. June can set in hot and heavy sometimes, but this year it was holding off on the worst of the humidity, with sunny mornings and breezy afternoons.

And who doesn't want to walk down Commercial Street when it's nice out? Even though the sidewalks and the street itself were filled with lanyard-wearing visitors—no one who comes here ever thinks of the street as anything but a pedestrian thoroughfare to which they are supremely entitled—there was still room enough to walk without actually bumping into someone. Until they stopped short right in front of you, that is, a curious mode of perambulation generally practiced by groups of people who clearly operate under the principle that no one else matters.

Okay, so even a perfect day can't completely take away my cynicism. But I've earned it. I didn't want to count how many years I'd lived here and done the P'town dance, moving from two thousand people in the winter to sixty thousand in the summer. Once you live with that for a while, you have the right to complain. And if you never plan to leave… well, then who's the one whose head should be examined?

Which brought me, appropriately enough, to Mirela; I was passing the gallery that sells her work. Not hers exclusively, but pretty much most people come there exclusively for her. Her style has changed from tame pretty landscapes to vibrant abstractions that make you want to respond in some way; the viewer is never merely an observer to Mirela's art. She's delighted when people say they loved her work. She's equally delighted when they say they hate it. I stood for a moment looking at the two pieces in the window, how they drew in the eye, how they didn't let go of the viewer. Even knowing Mirela, her pieces had that effect on me. I couldn't imagine this art colony without her distinctive flair.

I couldn't imagine this town without her, period.

For a moment I let myself hold the thought. No long coffee breaks at the Canteen, her favorite haunt, blessedly open year-round. None of the walks in the dunes she talked me into, when I followed her, huffing and puffing, until we scaled the last one and there before us in all its wild desperate splendor was the ocean. No more wine dinners at Ciro and Sal's. No more funny words of endearment. No more Mirela.

I had to acknowledge what I hadn't been seeing, that our friendship was lopsided at best. Mirela knows my past, my present, my aspirations. She's the one I turn to when I'm scared, or sick, or hurting. And I never even noticed that she wasn't doing the same. That she was doing most of the listening.

How could she have a sister I didn't know about? There was this whole life she'd left behind back in Bulgaria. To be fair, I had asked her about it. When we first met I found her exotic and interesting, and as Provincetown is inundated with Bulgarians every summer, I was anxious to find out more about the country, the culture. Mirela obliged; she could have worked for the tourist board. She told me about mountains and beaches, cities and resorts.

She told me stories. Maybe that was what had fascinated me the most. Maybe she'd seen that and used them to keep my mind where she wanted it to go. "When God decided to give away pieces of land to the people on earth," Mirela had said, her voice becoming almost singsong, "the Bulgarian was working hard in the field and was the last person who went to take his piece. And he was too late! God had already given away all the land there was. God thought hard what to give to the Bulgarian, but there was nothing left. So since the Bulgarian was famous for his kindness, modesty, and hard work, God decided to give

him a piece of his own land. He gave him a
piece of heaven, and that is Bulgaria."

"Tell me another."

Mirela was gently amused. "What, sunshine, are you writing a book of Bulgarian
folktales?

"They're better stories than we have
here."

"You like wine," said Mirela. "I will tell
you a story about wine in my country. Long
ago, Khan Krum decided there would be no
more wine in the land, because the people he
had defeated drank too much and became
soft. All vineyards were eradicated and every
person in whose property the forbidden liquid
was discovered, they were strangled."

It sounded like the beginning of most fairy
stories. Maybe there is such a thing as a collective unconscious, after all, I thought.

We were sitting at the Canteen, each appropriately enough with a glass of wine in
front of us, waiting for the Bulgarian salad
Rob Anderson made especially for Mirela. "A
poor widow named Ilaya was forced to raise
her son in great poverty," Mirela said. "Her
vineyard gave her valuable fruits. The woman
decided that since anyway she will lose the
vineyard, at least she can keep its last fruits.

She picked up the grapes, hid them in a pot next to the oven, and each day gave the fruit to her child. A lot of days passed by, and one day Ilaya realized that she made wine by accident. Cold, famine, and pestilence wearied the people the next winter. Ilaya didn't fear the cold, because every day she drank a small portion from the miracle wine."

My kind of peasant, I thought, sipping my own miracle wine as she spoke.

"In those days, Khan Krum kept lions, which he valued greatly. One was found dead. The khan promised that anyone who goes to him and acknowledges he did it, will receive a big reward. To know if he tells the truth, the person must also tear a hair from the beard of the khan." She looked up at me. "Some of the people in this story are very stupid," she acknowledged.

"I think they're supposed to be," I said. "It's a trope in fairy tales. Go on. What happened?"

Back to the singsong voice. "Lured by the award, about ten men went to the palace. But instead of receiving a reward, each of them was beaten up. To the great surprise of the people, the young son of Ilaya managed to pull out a hair from the grey beard of the khan. The boy told him how he was grown, that is, thanks to what he had such extraordinary power. Then Khan Krum ordered: If this grape has given you such courage, from now on it will be the new vineyard of the state. The grapes and the wine will be named Mavrud to remember your bravery. Such heroes are needed in the Bulgarian army!"

"Great," I commented. "So now you have drunken soldiers."

She looked at me sharply. "Do not doubt what this story teaches us," she said. "Through many years of repression, we keep what is important to us. No matter what they tell us to do, we manage to take care of ourselves. Under the Khans. Under Communism. We do what we have always done."

"You never lived in Bulgaria when it was still part of the Soviet Union, did you?"

"Sunshine," said Mirela gently, almost pityingly, "We were never part of the Soviet Union. Allies only."

Maybe it started there. Maybe my profound ignorance about her country—and the fact I'd never even bothered to look anything up, to test my assumptions—maybe all that was why she hadn't told me more about herself. Maybe it was all my fault. Insensitive. Uncaring.

I was still standing in front of the gallery and I blinked away the sudden tears. If she came back, I promised myself, that would change. I'd be a better friend. I'd ask the right questions.

If she came back.

12

Whaler's Wharf was bustling.

They'd taken down the police tape—or most of it; some still hung forlornly in tatters, moving sluggishly with the breeze. If you didn't *know*, I thought, you wouldn't know.

I had time before the lecture so I wandered down to the rotunda and through it, out onto the beach where the old Provincetown Theater chunks had ended up as Brett's final starring backdrop. I was standing there staring at them when I sensed someone behind me. "Hey, Sydney."

I turned around. It was Ben DeRuyter, who owns Whaler's Wharf, tall and good-looking and ridiculously young. He was contemplating the stones too. "Hey, Ben," I said.

"I'm sorry about Brett Falcone," he said. "You married him this week, didn't you?"

I shrugged. "We hosted the wedding," I said. "Lady Di was the officiant."

He nodded. "Poor guy," he said. "Right in the middle of the best part. He had everything."

Except a life, I thought, then was visited by a sudden streak of brilliance. "You know this place better than anyone else," I said eagerly, almost accusingly. "You'd know this. Tell me how someone got a body out here on a fine June evening without anyone seeing them do it." That had to be key; I knew from Julie as well as from the news reports that there weren't any witnesses. The state police were urging people to come forward if they'd seen anything. So far, no takers. "He was at the film society cocktail party alive and then he was back here, dead."

I expected him to be as clueless as the rest of us. Instead, he cleared his throat and said, a little diffidently, "Well, actually, there are a couple of options."

I stared at him. "What? How?" He seemed hesitant, and I was immediately impatient. "Come on, Ben, you must've already said all this to the police. And you know for starters it wasn't me who did any of this. I'm just trying to find out what might have happened." And as he hesitated, I said again, "Come on, you know me!"

"I know your *reputation*," he said, a little warily.

Miss Marple to the rescue, I thought. "Well, then, you know if I figure anything out, I do something helpful with it," I said. "If you tell me anything they can use, of course I'll tell the police." And as he still hesitated, "So *tell me*. Tell me for Brett's sake. You know you want to. What are the options? How did he do it?"

"You're right about it being a him, for starters," Ben said.

"Okay. Why?"

"You'd need a lot of strength," said Ben. "So here are the options." Once he'd decided to tell me, he was all in. "Wait. Why don't I just show you?"

"Absolutely!" I knew Whaler's Wharf was filled with nooks and crannies; I just didn't know where they all were. And I didn't have my purloined key anymore to go exploring on my own. Besides, once in a while, it's good to do things *right*.

Ben set off back into the building at a brisk pace. "So coming straight through here isn't the best option," he said, with a sweeping gesture encompassing the rotunda and the whole first floor. "Too many people here, even people up there who could be watching." He pointed above us, to the two balcony levels where anyone could be looking down on the main floor at any time.

"I'm with you there," I said.

We'd reached the front of the building where the elevator and staircases on either side allowed access to the upper floors. I followed him over to the east side and we went up to the first landing where he unlocked and opened a big metal door. "Another option," he said, holding it open and letting me see. "The alleyway."

"Right," I said. I'd already been there once before. My friend Chip the accountant was used to coming in this way every morning; he'd told me he always saw a number of miniature nips bottles strewn around the alley, detritus from the night's activities—the day after the night before. It was indeed a straight shot out to the sand and the harbor, but not especially private; ungated at either end, anyone could easily glance down at the wrong time.

"Not a great option, either," acknowledged Ben as if reading my mind. "So those
are the two he wouldn't use."

This was intriguing. "Are you going to
show me one he *might* have?" I asked.

He nodded. We crossed the main wharf
thoroughfare and he unlocked another unmarked door, this one leading down into the
basement.

Here were the storage cages Chip had
showed me before, one for every business,
some carefully padlocked and filled with
items, others a mess of broken and half-for-
gotten objects, locks hanging off or even ab-
sent. Weird stuff around: a rusty adding
machine, a child's ancient sled. "The old boiler
room," Ben said, opening another door. "It
used to be hotter than Hades down here when
they were all going. Cost a fortune. I thought
I'd put the oil company out of business when
we switched." He gestured toward what I took
to be the back of the building, if my orienta-
tion wasn't misleading me, which it could well
have done. "And there's number three," he
said, pointing to yet another unmarked door.

"What is it?"

He moved past me, unlocked the door,
and swung it open. It looked like something

out of a dystopian movie: a long tunnel stretching out away from us, wires and conduits and other mysterious gadgets running along the walls. "The tunnel goes all the way to the back of the building, under the rotunda," said Ben. "There's another one, another tunnel like this one, over on the other side."

You couldn't stand up in it, I thought, but you could still move along it reasonably comfortably if you bent over far enough, even dragging an inert body. I could see why Ben had said it would need to be a man; you'd need a lot of strength to get someone through there. I couldn't imagine myself managing it, for one. But sometimes people do extraordinary things for extraordinary reasons.

"And," Ben was saying, almost as if presenting a *piece de résistance*, "there are a couple of trap doors from the first floor that open down into them." That made sense: maintenance would need access and no one would want to go the whole length carrying tools and whatnot.

Or, for that matter, a dead body.

"That was three," said Ben cheerfully. He seemed jazzed by the puzzle element of our search, which was good; other people might find it ghoulish. "And the last one?" I asked, because that seemed to be what he wanted me to say.

"This way!" Back up onto the main floor, and then on the west staircase, up and up, past the cinema, past the studios and the offices, up a smaller flight of stairs that ended at a ladder affixed to the wall and a trap door that opened up. "Hope you have a head for heights," said Ben as he unlocked it and pushed it open.

I followed him up the ladder. I had no idea whether or not I had a head for heights. I'd been to the top of the Pilgrim Monument, of course, but looking straight out to the ocean isn't quite the same as looking down the side of a building. This investigation gig wasn't for the faint of heart.

Up on the roof (and how could I not have *that* song running through my mind all day, now?), the view was pretty damned good, the harbor stretching out as blue as the sky above it, dotted with sailboats and sports fishing boats. Behind me, the bustle of the outside dining patio at the Crown & Anchor; over to the right, the steeple of the Unitarian-Universalist meeting house. And between where we stood and the back end of Whaler's Wharf...

"He could do it here," I said, nodding. "Have to be careful," Ben agreed, "but it works for sure. We're high up enough that chances are good no one would see him. There are a couple of obstacles to get over, there." He pointed to where the roof rose in points punctuating the building design. "Have to be careful, yeah, but it's been done. *I've* done it. Then just follow the circular shape of the rotunda, and you're home free. Below you is the third-floor apartment, with Ross' Grill right under that. You could maybe throw him off the roof, but if it were me, I'd just pull him down onto the deck that goes with the apartment, there. It's second-home owners: no one's there now. Actually, they're hardly ever around."

I looked around me. "It would work," I said slowly, nodding. Then a thought occurred. "But it's locked! Who would have the key to get up here?"

"I'll let you in on a secret," said Ben. "This key?" He tossed it in the air and caught it again. "It opens every door in Whaler's Wharf. The storage areas. The basement. The restrooms." He paused. "The roof," he said.

"The same key I—" I stopped.

He was laughing. "Don't worry. Everyone in town probably has the key," he said. "Anyone who's ever worked here. Anyone who's ever known anyone who's worked here. At one time there were enough keys floating around to sink the fleet." He paused, thinking. "I don't know how someone from outside the community would have one, or know that it opens everything, but I can't imagine they couldn't find out. If you dislike someone enough to kill them, then you're probably ready to put some thought into the plan."

As someone clearly had. I took a last look around—it was a novel view of my town, and I have to say I was enjoying it—and climbed a little reluctantly down the ladder.

"So there are two options," I said as we regained the main floor. "He could get down into the basement area and take Brett through the tunnels."

"Dead or alive?"

"What?" I was startled.

"Well, it would have been a lot easier either way for Brett to still be alive," Ben pointed out. He was getting very good at this detective thing. "Instead of having to drag the body, if he could have gotten Brett along the tunnel—or over the roof, whichever route

205

he'd decided on—under his own steam, it would have been a lot faster and a lot easier."

"Good point." But Brett hadn't been shot, and you can't hold an award statue pointing at someone in quite the same way you might point a gun to force them to do something. Still, it was a very good point.

And the knowledge that the same key opened all the doors in Whaler's Wharf? That pretty much took care of Caroline Cooper in the locked bathroom, too. All they needed was one key and the knowledge that it opened every door.

At least now I knew *how*, but I still wasn't getting any closer to the elusive *who*.

I started to leave Ben, then turned back. "I don't suppose," I said a little diffidently, "that you'd loan me a key? Just for a little while? You can trust me, I'll get it back to you." At some point I might want to take a closer look at all those supposedly restricted areas.

He laughed. "Sooner you than half the people who have them," he said, and produced another key from his pocket. "Here you go."

"Thanks, Ben." That time I really left and headed into the film society's main room where Austin and Justin would be giving their talk. I wanted the killer to be Austin so badly I could almost taste it. Maybe there was some way I could find out if he had a copy of the key, too.

There were already people there, milling about, finding their places, chatting, all with lanyards and smiles alike firmly in place. The sudden deaths of two of their colleagues certainly hadn't ruined their days. Gretchen Callender fluttered in, caught sight of me, decided she couldn't pretend she hadn't, and came over. "Sydney! How nice to see you. I didn't know you were coming." She looked pointedly at my chest, which was free of lanyard or ticket-case.

"Special invitation," I said, my smile no doubt as false as hers.

"I see," she said. "Such a terrible thing, of course…"

I nodded. Two deaths. A terrible thing. "It doesn't seem to have made anyone lose their enthusiasm, though."

Gretchen dismissed my thought with a wave of her hand. "Sydney, people plan their whole *year* around this festival! We can't disappoint them!"

I thought that perhaps she was giving P'town a little too much credit, but managed not to say it. Toronto, yes. Cannes, for sure. Sundance, a must. But *Provincetown*? "No, of course not," I said in apparent agreement. "Maybe you can start a scholarship in their names, some kind of grant to aspiring film producers."

"Of course, of course, we've already thought of that," she said in a voice that assured me she hadn't thought of that. "And we're already making plans. We'll see they're remembered, Sydney, never fear. As soon as this craziness is over! But it's all going terribly well, isn't it, other than that?"

Other than that, Mrs. Lincoln, how was your evening at the theater? "Um, sure," I said uncertainly. "Gretchen, you know Austin Hyde—"

"Of course I do," she interrupted briskly. "Austin and I go way back."

Of course they did. "I'm wondering if he knew in advance about Brett's award. Like if he were on some sort of nominating committee or something." Okay, so I was clutching at straws. I was ready to clutch at anything.

Gretchen looked at me blankly. "Austin? On a nominating committee?" she asked. "Well, he was part of the poll, of course, but so were a lot of other people, Austin wasn't there specially or anything. We polled a lot of industry insiders. But once we knew Brett was coming, of course we wanted to do something special for him."

I suspected it was the other way around, that she'd decided to do something special to lure him to P'town. Never mind. One way or another, Austin was probably on board and had had plenty of time to plan whatever nefarious deeds he wanted.

Breathe, Riley, I cautioned myself. *Just breathe. He's not guilty just because you want him to be.* "Who financed it?" I asked.

Gretchen frowned. Already she was looking over my shoulder, preparing her best and brightest smile, ready to greet the Beautiful People as they arrived. "What?"

"Brett's lifetime achievement award," I said. "Who financed it?" You don't rent Town Hall for nothing. You don't create a new award out of thin air. And I was willing to bet that there had been an envelope that changed hands along with the trophy.

Gretchen seemed to realize who she was talking to. "That's private information, Sydney," she said. "And now you'll have to excuse me." She brushed by me and was already saying, "Clark, darling," before I had time to react.

It didn't matter. Everyone and their Aunt Edna had known Brett would be coming to P'town, getting married, receiving the award. How did you narrow that down to the one person who wanted him dead?

And why, oh why, did anyone want him dead at all?

13

Ali texted me just before the talk began. *There's something going on with Ellie.* I glanced around automatically before answering. *Like what?*

Like she doesn't want to come out of her room. Says she's being followed. Says she needs to go back home. She's scared.

Ellie being followed? How did that enter into anything? I thought for a moment and then texted, *Do you believe her?* Ali's generally pretty good at determining when someone's telling the truth—or not. I've never been able to lie to him, not without him knowing exactly what I'm doing. Maybe it's a law enforcement thing. Maybe it's just an Ali thing.

The answer came back quickly. *I believe she believes it.*

I wanted to take the phone outside and actually have a conversation with him, but Justin and Austin—and didn't that sound like some sort of performing duo?—were getting ready to start, and, besides, I didn't want to give up my seat. *Try and find out what's going on,* I texted. *I'll be there as soon as Justin's talk's over.*

I'd stationed myself toward the back and on the end of a row so I could observe without seeming obvious. And the gang was all here: Rob Francis right in the front row supporting his client; Lou Estrada and Brian the pain-in-the-neck personal assistant together looking suitably mournful and surreptitiously checking out the crowd—only less subtly than I was.

I considered Ali's text. First was the fact of Ellie being there rather than here; I'd expected the three of them to arrive together. She was a little ditzy and a little strange but she clearly loved her brother, and if there were ever a time for her to support him, this was it. So why was she at the inn?

And who would want to follow her? She'd come in during the third act, so to speak, arriving after the action, once all the violence was over. She hadn't been here when either Caroline or Brett was killed. Who could wish her harm? Or was she just imagining things?

She hadn't seemed the most stable pixie in the forest.

With some effort I tried to focus on what was happening in the room. Austin was talking. "And in a situation like that, it's all hands on deck to get the work done," he said. I wished I'd been listening so I knew what he was talking about. "*Revenge* almost didn't make it here to Provincetown, but of course we're all glad it did. And if I may say so, it's a fitting tribute to its lead actor, who unfortunately might win an Oscar posthumously." Applause in the room, everyone looking suitably impressed.

Justin cleared his throat. "Brett would have liked to add a few things here," he said, and suddenly you could have heard a pin drop. "I wish he were the one to say it, but I know it's what he planned." Another pause, and the beginnings of tension telegraphed from person to person. I leaned slightly forward. "The truth is," said Justin, "Brett was stepping back from involvement in films like *Revenge*, and it was largely because of his experiences with this particular production team." Someone gasped. Rob Francis looked like he was about to faint.

Jeannette de Beauvoir

"*Revenge* was never supposed to be a money-maker, and I know how sacrilegious that is to say in Hollywood, but someone has to say it. Films like *Revenge* are supposed to reveal the heart and soul of everyone involved. They're about communicating something deep and meaningful to the audience, not raking in cash at the box office. But every day we struggled to make it the picture it was meant to be, and every day we were up against too much pressure for it to be something it wasn't. What Austin hasn't told you is that *Revenge* barely made it into this film festival. *Revenge* barely got completed at all. There were rewrites every night. There were takes and retakes and even more retakes, so it ended up with overage everywhere—on time, on money, on the precious work and heart that some of us put into it."

He paused, his eyes traveling slowly around the room until they came to rest on Rob Francis. "I have a decade and a half of experience in the industry," Justin said. "Brett had even more than that. And we were sickened by it, what it's become. We thought we were making one last great film together. And what I'm grieving today isn't just my partner, my husband, the love of my life. I'm grieving that creative collaboration we wanted so much and now won't ever have."

Austin was starting to recover from the shock. He cleared his throat. "I should add—clarify, really—that what happened on the set of *Revenge* was no different from—"

Justin cut him off. "Austin, you and Caroline drove that story straight off a cliff. And when we needed help, when we turned to the people who were supposed to represent us, who supposedly had our best interests at heart, and I'm talking about you, Rob, and you, Lou, well, we saw what side of the issue they were aligned with."

I pulled out my phone and texted Ali. *Justin's just committed professional suicide.*

Gretchen stood up from where she'd been sitting in the front row and began applauding. "Justin, what a refreshing sideline to the film! I'm sure the hearts of everyone here go out to you in this difficult time. Ladies and gentlemen, Justin Braden and Austin Hyde! Let's all give them both a big round of applause and heartfelt thanks for—"

Justin said, "I'm not finished."

Austin was trying to keep himself from laughing; I wasn't the only one to label it suicide. "Yes," he said to Justin. "I think you'll find that you are."

***

I wasn't leaving Justin alone, not after that. I got Mike on the phone while people were still clapping and starting to talk excitedly, in stage whispers and more, about what they'd just seen. "Can you get the car to Whaler's Wharf right now?"

"What's going on?"

"Justin's imploded. I need to get him out of here."

"Okay. I can do ten minutes."

That was ten minutes longer than Justin could survive with this lot, I diagnosed. "Okay. Pick us up at the bookshop. I'll bring him over there." The Provincetown Bookshop was nearby, on the other side of Commercial Street, and it doesn't have an extensive film section; maybe that would keep some of the lanyards away.

I reached Justin without too much ado. Austin was smirking up a storm. I restrained myself—with some effort—from actually kicking him, and grabbed Justin's arm instead. "Come on, we're getting out of here."

"I had to say it," he said.

"Okay. But we're still getting out of here."

Austin said, "If you think you're ever working in Hollywood again, you'd better think twice. You're blacklisted, boy." His threatening words would have sounded tougher if he'd had an actor's voice; he'd have looked more menacing without that ridiculous soul patch. But there was still something, something dark going on behind his ridiculous façade, and I had a feeling it wasn't just about Justin and his implosion. There was something there that made me suddenly want to keep him away from Mike. Maybe violence does beget violence. I thought of a couple of cutting things to say, but decided not to waste my time. Better to regroup and, please God, prove Austin a killer.

We were halfway down the stairwell when we met Julie coming up. "No," I said at once.

"I need to speak with Mr. Braden," she said crisply.

Behind us, the gossip machine was pouring out through the film society doors. "Not here, Julie," I implored her. "Please."

She seemed to notice them for the first time. "What is this?"

217

"It was Justin's swan song. Can we do this someplace else?"

She surprised me. "Okay. The rotunda. Now."

Julie getting soft? No time to marvel; I grabbed Justin again and propelled him along the second-floor walkway to the back of the building, calling Mike on the way.

"Race Point Inn."

"Mike," I said. "Change of plans. We don't need the car, thanks anyway. See you later." I clicked off before he could ask me anything. Besides, I had a lot to ask *him*, actually, starting with why he'd married Austin in the first place, and going on to whether he shared my suspicions about his ex. No time; not now.

We went down and around the curving staircase to the bottom of the rotunda, where Julie had appropriated one of the benches facing the fountain. "Thanks, Julie." I still wasn't sure why she was doing it, but no need to look a gift horse in the mouth.

"All right." She wasn't going to unwind so much as to smile. "We received some information we'd like to ask you about," she said to Justin.

He seemed to wake up. "What information?"

She pulled out her notebook and consulted it. "Do you know someone named Roger Best?"

He stiffened immediately. "Why?"

"Just answer the question," she said. "Do you know Roger Best?"

Justin nodded. "Yeah."

"And can you tell me in what context?" She was asking him questions, but she already knew the answers. I could see that.

"He used to date my husband," he said, a little stiffly.

"I see." Yep; she already knew. "And when was the last time you saw him?"

Justin was frowning. "Why are you asking about Roger?"

"Who is he?" I asked, not caring which of them responded. "What does he have to do with anything?"

Julie surprised me again by answering. "We received information this morning that Roger Best had made arrangements to see Brett Falcone during the film festival, and that they were planning to spend time together." She was watching Justin.

"That's ridiculous," I said automatically.

"It could be true," said Justin.

We both stared at him. He shrugged. "Justin and Roger go way back," he said, and I remembered being in the war room in Glenn's office, and someone talking about this old boyfriend as a possible motive for Justin to kill Brett. Who had brought it up?

Justin was still talking. "Look, they were lovers, yeah. And I'm not kidding myself that there wasn't still something there. But it just doesn't matter." He sounded exhausted. "Don't you see? It doesn't matter. I'm the one Brett chose to spend his life with. I'm the one he married. Next to that—that commitment, that kind of love—I could deal with indiscretions, I could deal with Roger. Brett always wanted everything. That expression—have your cake and eat it, too? That could've been coined for Brett. But I didn't care. I had the part of him that was the most important." He drew in a long, deep breath. "So Roger's here. So what?"

I said to Julie, "Doesn't it feel oddly *convenient* to you that every time it seems Justin isn't the focus of the investigation, something new and shiny gets dropped in your lap? It's almost as if someone really wanted him to get arrested and stay arrested."

"Yes," she said, her eyes still on Justin. "I've been thinking that, too."

"It was an email?" I asked.

She nodded. Julie in an expansive mood. I almost wanted to take a picture, to freeze the frame for all eternity. "Anonymous. Someone out there's showing off their mad hacking skills."

Justin said, "Is this real? Is someone actually trying to set me up?"

I bit my lower lip and looked at Julie. We'd none of us phrased it that baldly, but after the speech he'd just given, I wasn't surprised that Justin was able to cut to the chase.

Julie said, "It's what we may be starting to think." She looked at him with some speculation. "So let's think about this, Mr. Braden. Who hates *you* so much they'd set you up for murder?"

Whoa. She was right. That changed the calculations altogether. I started going through the list of people I was already thinking of as the usual suspects... Austin? Rob? Lou? Brian? Someone I hadn't even met, yet?

Justin said, blankly, "No one. No, really. I've never done anything that I know of to hurt anyone..."

"Well," said Julie, putting her notebook away and standing up, "if I were you, I'd have a good hard think about it. Really, really imagine who might feel that strongly about you. That's a lot of hatred to be carrying around." She paused. "And there's no reason to think it's going to stop now."

I remembered thinking that about Caroline: whatever had started there hadn't finished there.

By the time we wandered back through the building the cinema crowd had dispersed, no doubt eager to get online or on the phone back to LA, be the first to break the news, serve the dish about Justin's public unraveling. Plus, the afternoon films were all starting, and this bunch didn't miss a showing. We started back east along Commercial Street, Justin getting stronger and stronger by the minute. "I can't believe it," he said. "I can't believe someone wants to do that to me."

"Who would?" I was trotting to keep up with him. "Can you think of anybody?"

"Who would?" he echoed. "How'd you like to be asking yourself who might want to see you locked up for life—oh!" He stopped dead and I barreled into him. So did the tourist coming up fast on our heels.

I ignored her muttering. "You know who," I said. "You know! Justin! Who is it?"

He shook his head. "Probably not," he said. "I'm probably wrong. And it couldn't be, anyway."

"Stop being so mysterious," I complained. We were in front of the library by then, the flow of people walking down the street moving around us, and not very gracefully. "Come inside," I said, inspired, and led him up the walkway to the main entrance. "We can have a little privacy here."

Let it be said, now and never to be forgotten, that the Provincetown Public Library absolutely rocks. We're the only library I can imagine with a half-scale model of a fishing schooner smack dab in the middle of it, rising up two floors. If you didn't know you were by the ocean, the model of the Rose Dorothea would tell you so.

Justin looked like he was somewhere else. Like maybe doing sums in his head, or something. "Come on," I urged him, and propelled him up the stairs. At the top of the third floor is one of my favorite places in town, a big window overlooking the harbor with comfortable chairs in front of it. Not everybody knows about this space; it's near the poetry section, and apparently most people don't come looking for poetry. The comfy chairs were available, and I sat Justin right down in one and pulled the other one closer. Outside, you could see the water, the cormorants out on the breakwater opening their wings to dry in the sun, the sudden blast of a ship's horn, one of the whale-watch boats heading out.

"All right," I said to Justin. "Tell me what's going on."

He was staring. "Why is there a ship in here?"

"Never mind that now. Tell me!"

He said, "There's only one person in my whole life you could say I harmed, and I didn't really—well, not intentionally. It wasn't personal."

I wanted to give him a good shake. "Who? What did you do unintentionally?"

He met my eyes. His were guileless. "I already told you," said Justin. "I testified against him in court, and the jury found him guilty."

I remembered now. Nighttime along Commonwealth Avenue in the Back Bay, moneyed residents who didn't all draw their curtains and draperies at night, just because. They were who they were and the rest of the world could take a running leap at itself. Justin, walking his mother's dog in the dark, stopping to wait for the dog to pee. Looking in the window with nothing more than a mild desultory curiosity. Seeing the argument, maybe hearing the screams and the yelling through the glass. Watching in horror as the man pulled out a gun and shot his wife. Justin standing there, the dog forgotten, not believing what he'd seen. No wonder he hated Boston. "The domestic incident," I said, unconsciously phrasing it the way Julie would. "You think he blames you?"

"I can't think of anyone else," Justin said. "Listen, it was all so appalling. Bad enough to *see* it—you see something like that, you know, you can't un-see it again. It's there forever. I went home, and got back into work, and Brett kept telling me it was all going to be all right—oh, God!" He stared at me, his eyes wild. "If we're right—if I'm right—then I'm the one who got Brett killed! Oh, God!"

"Stop it," I said, and then, as that didn't work, I grabbed his hands and forced them together and held them in place. "Stop it *now*," I said, as severely as I could. "That has nothing to do with you." Well, it did, actually, I could see his point, but having him fall apart because of guilt wasn't going to help anyone. "Listen

225

to me, Justin. If this is him—and you don't know for sure it is—but if it is, it's all on him. He's a killer. Not you."

"He's obsessed with me," Justin said. "I knew it before."

"What?" I let go of his hands. "What are you talking about?"

He looked thoroughly miserable. "After I went back home, after the trial," he said. "I—we—started getting letters. Real letters, you know? The kind nobody writes anymore, everyone uses email now. But these were real letters."

"Okay," I said.

"They were threatening, sure," he said, a lot more calmly than I'd have said it. I've gotten threatening letters in my time, and I knew exactly how it felt. Like the floor had suddenly disappeared and you were fast-tracked into some subterranean darkness. "But the prosecutor in Boston, he'd talked to me about it when I was there. Because… Oh, God," he said again. He was breathing way too fast.

"Put your head between your knees," I said quickly. I can recognize a panic attack when I see one. "You're hyperventilating, Justin. Head down… like that. Breathe with me.

In… and out… Good, do it again, in… and out."

He got it back under control. By then I'd marshaled my thoughts. "Why didn't you get anonymity when you testified?" I asked.

"There wasn't any reason to. Apparently these situations—the violence is really only aimed at one person, the one they're in a relationship with. It's not a random bad guy. So there wasn't any concern. It wasn't until after I testified… when he heard me, and they said I was part of the movie industry, I don't even know why they should mention that in court, it didn't have anything to do with why I was out on Comm. Ave. that night… but they did, anyway, and he went wild." He paused. "The prosecutor said that probably nothing would happen, he had years to spend in prison, a lot could happen in that time. But he said it wouldn't be unusual for there to be letters. That's all they have in there, is time."

"Was he at Sousa-Baranowski?" Supermax.

Justin nodded. "So the letters came, and they were pretty rough. Pretty awful. I started reading them, but then Brett got hold of one and put a stop to it. He kind of lost it, actually." He smiled at the memory. "My knight in shining armor." The image shimmered between us for a moment before dissipating. Justin sighed. "Brian dealt with them after that."

Brian, the Obnoxious Personal Assistant. I nodded. "Did they really continue? For years? How long was this guy in for, anyway?" Maybe too many questions at once. *Slow down, Riley. Breathe.*

"I think they went on for a while. I don't know for how long. Probably not recently, but I don't know. I can't say I was really paying attention. You know, out of sight, out of mind. Listen, Sydney, this might be nothing. I don't even know if the guy's out of prison."

"Aren't they supposed to notify you if he is?"

"That's victims," he said. "Not witnesses."

"Hell." I thought for a moment. "We have to tell Ali. He can help with this." But even as I was saying it, I was connecting the dots. Ali's text about Ellie. *Says she's being followed.* And then, *I believe she believes it.* I turned to Justin. "Was your sister in court when you testified?"

"What? Ellie? Why?"

"Just tell me," I urged.

"Yeah, she was. I didn't want to—I didn't feel I could—" He stopped floundering, seemed to pull himself together. "Brett couldn't come East with me," he said. "They'd postponed the trial twice. Both of those times he'd arranged his life so he could be with me. When the date was set, finally, he was in the middle of shooting something in South Africa. He couldn't get away." He took another gulp of air. "I hate Boston," he confessed. I didn't tell him I already knew. "I hated growing up there. Always felt isolated. Got some bullying. And my father…" His voice trailed off until he visibly, again, got hold of himself. "I went to BU, sure, but got out the minute I could. I didn't even go to graduation. I just wanted to be as far from Boston as I could get. And every time I came back, it was like being sixteen all over again." Another breath; he was close to hyperventilating again. "And then suddenly here I was coming back for something even worse than anything I'd ever experienced before. Ellie was so young… but she wanted to come, and I let her. She sat in—I don't know what you call it, the audience?—and looked right at me the whole time, and I looked right at her, and it got me through. She was what got me through." Another pause. "Why? Why did you ask that?"

"Because," I said carefully, "I think he's here, in P'town, and I think Ellie's seen him."

14

I called Ali. Never mind that I was in a library: desperate times call for desperate measures. "Are you still with Ellie?"

"And hello to you, too," said Ali. "Yes, oddly enough, I am. We're at the inn. And it's a very good place for you to avoid at the moment, *cara*. Your friend Justin is pretty much *persona non grata* around here for a while. What on earth did he do at that presentation, anyway?"

I glanced at Justin. He was scrolling through texts on his phone. "He—well, he kind of lost it. Said some stuff that was noble and true and very impressive—*and* is pretty much guaranteed to keep him from ever working in the film industry again."

Justin looked up at me, sharply, but didn't say anything.

Ali whistled. "That explains it, then. Austin Hyde's here and raising a ruckus, to put it mildly. Talking lawyers and lost revenue and I don't even know what else. I'm starting to think *he's* a little unhinged, to tell the truth. There's something going on with him. Anyway. apparently Justin put his nose out of joint."

"You can say that again," I said.

"He probably deserved it," said Ali cheerfully. "He hasn't been exactly courteous to your boss, either."

"Mike? Why? What's he doing to Mike?" I felt like a lioness when something threatens her cub. Or is it kitten? But I'd been feeling something off, there; and I owed Mike a great deal, aside from him being generally very nice and absolutely not deserving of any criticism. Like the fact he'd once saved my life.

"Austin has minions," Ali answered, a little obliquely.

"What?" And why him? *I* want minions. I've always wanted minions.

"He's had people checking out the inn," said Ali. "Kids running around looking for violations."

"They won't find any," I said stoutly. "Everything's up to code. We run a tight

ship." A thought occurred. "Oh, my good-
ness, did he try to pull that in the kitchen? Tell
me he tried to pull that in the kitchen!" I'd
have paid good money to see Adrienne the
diva chef's reaction to Austin's snooping.

"No idea," said Ali. He'd finished with the
twin topics of Mike and Austin. "How's Justin
holding up? Ellie's here, and she wants to see
him."

"We're at the library," I said. "Any port in
a storm. Listen, Ali, I think I know who's setting Justin up."

"So do I," said Ali. "Rick Davies."

I realized I hadn't asked Justin for the
wife-beater's name, and this was one I didn't
recognize. "Hey," I said to Justin. "What was
that guy's name? The one you testified
against?"

"Rick Davies," said Justin.

"Rick Davies," said Ali at the same time.
"I just told you."

"Who the hell is Rick Davies?" I demanded. "Have you met this guy? Have you
even seen him?"

"I expect, *cara*," said Ali gently, "that he's
using a different name at the moment. Ellie
saw him last night when she was sitting at the
bar, she remembered that today, but the

233

restaurant was full of film people so it could have been anybody. And she's a little fuzzy on the details. She thought she saw him again, today, placed him and got scared. Before that, she just thought he looked vaguely familiar. Then she got the context. She isn't able to describe him, though."

"What do you mean, she can't describe him? She sat in court when Justin was testifying."

Ali gave an exaggerated sigh. "He's what she calls ordinary looking, with maybe brown hair but maybe not, no idea of his eye color, no distinguishing features. Could be anyone."

"No soul patch?" I asked plaintively. I don't give up easily.

"It's not Austin," said Justin.

"It's not Austin," said Ali.

"There's an echo chamber in here," I said. "All right. We're at the library, did I say? It's quiet here, why don't you come over?" I certainly didn't want to walk into Austin Hyde decrying Justin's speech in the lobby of the Race Point, or worse still, trying to pin something nefarious on Mike. I was annoyed enough that it wasn't him we were looking for; I'd probably want to deck him, given the proper provocation. And while he might not be good for Caroline's murder, it didn't mean he wasn't planning something else.

"Yeah, okay," said Ali. "Half an hour."

"Hasta la vista," I said and disconnected. I looked at Justin. "Are you okay?"

"I'm better," he said, and he actually looked it. "Now that I know what this is all about. That's such a weight lifted. I'd been thinking I was going crazy, I really had." He paused. "But Brett—"

"Don't go there right now," I said briskly. "We'll figure this out and the police will arrest him and then you can deal with your feelings." There was something nagging at me, something wrong about our headlong rush into solving the crime, something that we weren't seeing, weren't noticing, but I couldn't put my finger on it… Was it about Mike and Austin? About Ellie? Justin? Nope: I Wasn't getting anything. "Here," I said to Justin. "Come over and see the Rose Dorothea."

We wandered over to the railing. On this floor, we were about even with the top-ends of her masts, which disappeared up into the ceiling above us. "The Rose Dorothea was part of the Provincetown fishing fleet," I told Justin. It was a good story, and it would distract him.

"It's big, for a fishing boat," he said doubt-fully.

"It's a schooner," I said. "Typical of the time. The real one was twice this size, if you can imagine that. Anyway, the story is, in 1907 a trophy was offered by Sir Thomas Lipton of Lipton Tea fame for a Fishermen's Race in Massachusetts Bay. A couple of Provincetown boats were in it, and some from Gloucester, too—that's another fishing town, up the coast on the North Shore, and the two fleets were fiercely competitive. And this is it, the Rose Dorothea, the boat that won the Lipton Cup, even though toward the end of the race she lost part of her foremast, if you can believe that. Came limping into the harbor, but came limping in *first*. She was just that fast. The Lipton Cup's downstairs, in the main room of the library, it's quite something. You'll have to re-mind me to show you on the way out." We'd passed it on the way in, of course, but I wasn't trying to get Justin to relax then, I just wanted to get him someplace quiet. "And the race was never run again, so we've kept the Cup all these years." It would have been a better story, I thought, if Provincetown and Gloucester had kept up the races and the rivalry, but hey, the Cup's still pretty cool.

"Okay," said Justin. "Good story." He seemed to be really thinking about it, and I wondered for a moment if it would find its way into a future screenplay, then remembered it wasn't likely Justin would be writing any more of those. "But why's this in a *library?*"

"It wasn't always a library," I admitted. "It started out as a church, then for a while it housed Walter Chrysler's private art collection—he's the founder of the Chrysler corporation, did you ever have one of their cars?—and then after that it was a museum for years and years. And while it was still a museum—I want to say in 1977, but I'm not sure—that's when they built the boat. Flyer Santos, he only died a few years ago, actually—built it with a whole load of volunteers. He was a custom boat designer and master builder and owned Flyers Boat Yard for decades." Thus reminded, I wondered if once the film festival was over, my friend Thea and I would be able to get back to normal, rent the little nineteen-footer from Flyer's and again careen wildly around the harbor under sail. Having fun just for the sake of having fun seemed impossibly out of reach at the moment.

Justin seemed to pick up on my thoughts. "It feels like nothing's ever going to go back to normal," he said. "Even when I go home— Brett won't be there. The house…" He stopped for a moment, took a deep breath, steadied his voice. "I don't know *how* to be there, Sydney. I don't know how to do life without him."

I took his arm and led him back to the chairs in front of the window. "It'll be hard," I acknowledged. "But—and forgive me if I'm being indelicate, here—but you have enough money so you never need to work again. You must know that. Back there at Whaler's Wharf, you did a pretty thorough job of burning your Hollywood bridges." I paused, considered what I might say. The two couldn't be unconnected: people burn bridges for one of two reasons: either out of desperation—or because they know they have a boat moored nearby. "You don't have to go back there, back home. Oh, I don't mean stay *here*, you already hate Boston, and P'town's never going to be comfortable for you after all this. But you can go anywhere, Justin. You can reinvent yourself. Travel. Climb Everest, explore the Amazon, be on *America's Got Talent*. Be whoever you want to be." It was sounding pretty damned appealing to me, to tell the truth.

He looked at me, his face blank. "I don't know how to do any of that," he said. He sounded lost. I wondered if he really was.

It wasn't exactly the time to point out to him that he was young, gorgeous, and wealthy, either; it wouldn't take long for him to find someone else if that was what he wanted, or to learn how to live a life of ease on his own. Yeah, Brett was filling his mind and his heart and his soul right now—but a year from now? Five years from now?

Justin was going to be one supremely eligible bachelor.

Not the time, I reminded myself. He was in shock. He was in grief. And again I found myself wondering why it was me and Ali who had become his support system. The parents hadn't exactly rushed down to comfort him— okay, fair play to them, his mother had cancer, but that doesn't keep you from a phone call or a video conference. And it wasn't just the family: no friends from LA had flown out to be with him in his time of grief. I'd seen his Facebook feed when I was online looking at his laptop and there wasn't the dramatic

239

outpouring of support you expect in a forum where everyone has something to say about everything. No one here for the film festival seemed to give a fig about what happened to him, and that included his agent, whose fate was presumably tied to Justin's.

Actually, when you thought about it that way, Rob Francis seemed downright sinister.

But it couldn't be Rob any more than it could be Austin: Justin knew them, they'd been on the scene for years when presumably this Rick guy had been in supermax. It couldn't really be any of the satellites circling the money-making planets that were Brett Falcone and Justin Braden.

My phone vibrated and I checked the text. Mirela. *My sister is finished having this baby now,* she wrote.

I had no idea how to respond. Wonderful? Isn't it a little soon? Why are you in Plovdiv instead of P'town? I hope it all comes out okay? After a moment I typed, *Girl or boy?*

The answer came back almost immediately. *A girl.*

Lots of information there. *Has your sister named her?*

I am naming her.

Which only reinforced my greatest fears. Mirela was taking charge of this little person's life, and she wanted to raise her Bulgarian, so Mirela was staying in Bulgaria. Her niece would have the benefit of whatever extended family Mirela had—not that I knew what configuration said family took—and that was going to be that. It was a big city, a cultural center; she could be an artist there as easily as in Provincetown, any day of the week. It was completely depressing. I felt tears pressing against my eyes. *I'm sorry I haven't asked you about your family before,* I texted. *I've been a poor friend to you.*

Silence. Great. Then, *I am naming her Lilia. We will call her Lily.*

It's a beautiful name.

She is not beautiful. She looks like a very angry old man.

I grinned. That was closer to the Mirela I knew. *She'll grow out of it.*

We will hope you are correct. I must go now. Not for Mirela were the texting acronyms of TTYL or BRB. *Bye,* I texted, and thrust the phone back into my pocket. Mirela was going to be all right.

Was I?

***

"It's about figuring out who it is," said Ali. "So let's start with the basics. What do we know?" The question was rhetorical; I could recognize the signs. Ali often answers himself. "We know he had dinner at the Race Point restaurant last night."

There were four of us huddled up in the third floor of the library, our own war council. "Maybe he's staying at the inn," I suggested. "I can go through the reservations."

"Probably won't tell us anything. There's no way he'd use his own name."

"Okay. We know," I said, "that he's got decent coding skills. He sent emails the police couldn't trace."

"Good point," Ali acknowledged. "And?"

Ellie shivered. She was looking frail in jeans and an oversized t-shirt. She and Justin were sitting very close together, gripping each other's hands. I was glad to see it, glad there was someone in his life who cared. "I think he had gray hair," she said. "That would make sense, wouldn't it? He'd get older. He was in prison for ten years."

"Is that how long you figured?" I asked Justin. "Ten?" He nodded.

"Must have been a model prisoner," said Ali, frowning. "Unless the conviction was for manslaughter. Do you remember?"

Justin shook his head. "I testified, and I left," he said. "I felt soiled, somehow, just being in the same room as him. I couldn't get that night, that window, out of my head. I couldn't wait to get out of there. I was sitting at Logan Airport waiting to go home an hour after the judge let me go."

"And you weren't interested in following up?" I asked. "You didn't even just look it up, later?" Call me insatiably curious—or even snoopy—if you will, but that seemed a little off to me. Disingenuous, somehow. Something *that* significant happens and you don't even wonder about the outcome?

And if that were true, then how did he know Rick Davies had served ten years?

"Let's step back a minute," said Ali. He was watching me and was probably afraid something snarky was going to come out of my mouth. He's usually right about such things. "If we're right and it's this Davies character, then what's the endgame? Make sure Justin's locked up, like he thinks Justin locked him up? From what I've heard, everything around Justin's possible guilt is circumstantial."

"He does have a motive, though," I said, almost apologetically. Several of them, in fact.

Justin said, "The point is they can't prove any of it, because I didn't do it. And what's going to happen when he realizes I'm not the chief suspect anymore? If he did kill Caroline and Brett, if he came all this way to do this, what's he going to do now? Say, oh, well, nice try, and walk away?"

That was the question. One of them, anyway.

15

Justin should have some protection," I said to Ali that night.

He'd finally given in to my pleas and was cooking. I was sipping a Côtes du Rhône, scratching Ibsen under his chin, and mulling over what Nancy Drew, Girl Detective, would do in my place. And maybe the first thing was to make sure nobody else got killed.

An idea that had, hopefully, occurred to the police.

"He's got someone," said Ali. "Where's the garlic?"

"You mean the powder? In the spice rack."

He sighed. "Real garlic, *cara*. I brought it with me." And so he had; Ali trusts nothing about either my pantry or my skills.

"Just kidding, then," I said. "Who?"

"Who, what?" The room was starting to smell really good, and that was even without the garlic. I couldn't imagine what the next ten minutes would bring. "Who's watching him?" I asked, taking a swallow of wine.

"Julie's got someone. Staties don't have it in the budget."

"And Julie does?" That was a surprise.

"She finagled it somehow," Ali said. "And he's not staying at Race Point, either."

"If it were up to Justin, he'd have been on the first flight out," I said. "Listen, I've been thinking, don't you think it's a little weird he doesn't have any friends?"

"I don't have a lot of friends. That doesn't mean anything."

"You do, too," I said. "You have me, and Mirela, and Mike, and that guy you go running with, and Ned at your office. You even have Stephanie the Bra-less Wonder." Stephanie lived in Ali's building in Boston, and always managed to pop out her front door every time he was going in or out, asking for help with a leaky pipe or putting up a picture. He couldn't figure out if she was genuinely helpless or coming on to him. I had a pretty good idea which one it was. "But Justin doesn't seem to have anybody. And you'd think, moving in the social circles he and Brett moved it, he'd have a lot of people. I have the impression he was kind of friendly with Caroline, come to think of it. Maybe she was a friend."

"How do you know that? And where's the colander?"

"Under the oven. In that drawer thingie." I took a drink. Confession time. "So—I saw some of his emails to her."

That got him, as I knew it would. "You did what?"

"He'd left his laptop at the front desk," I said defensively. "And he was arrested then so I thought I could find something there that would say he was guilty or say he wasn't."

"Something that then couldn't be used in court." He tossed a dishcloth over his shoulder. "I swear sometimes I don't know what you're thinking."

"And there was no password, who doesn't have a password?"

"Obviously someone who doesn't expect other people to be going through their computer."

"Oh, please." Not my best-ever comeback. I drank some more wine. "Anyway, they seemed friendly enough, even though mostly they were talking about work. She thought

Brett was keeping Justin from being really creative."

"Was he?"

I shrugged. "Who knows?" If this really were a Miss Marple or Nancy Drew or Jessica Fletcher story, there would have been a neat reason for that exchange between them. But real life is, unfortunately, full of plot holes. "What are you making, anyway? It smells gorgeous."

"Smoked paprika steak and lentils with spinach," he said. "Cheese board, then lemon-berry savarin to finish."

"This must be what heaven smells like." My life is seriously excellent: my boyfriend is gorgeous, cooks like a top chef, and is smart on top of it all. What more could you want? Of course, I'm a pretty good catch, too. "So what's the plan, Agent Hakim?"

"Dinner, I thought, would be nice."

I threw a cushion at him. "You know what I mean."

"Sydney, we can't keep playing crime-stoppers here. I got involved because I thought Justin needed some support, but I'm not the investigating officer. I'm not even in the right investigating *agency*. Let's just get through the week without any more violence

and it'll be a success." He negotiated putting
food on plates. "And, you know, I wouldn't
mind catching a film or two myself."

I started laughing; I couldn't help myself.
"Good Lord, I'd kind of forgotten the whole
point of the festival!"

He helped me out of the couch and held
the chair for me and poured more wine in my
glass. "Bon appétit."

I clinked my glass with his ginger ale.
"Cheers. And thanks for this, Ali, it's amazing."

And we didn't talk about Justin or Hollywood or murder at all for the rest of the night.

***

Ali was as good as his word: he'd already
called Gretchen to get tickets to three screenings the next day. "How can you see three in
one day?" I asked. I knew for the festival-goers that was pretty much par for the course,
but I couldn't imagine Ali doing it.

"I want to see them all," he said, reasonably. "And you have to work, right?"

"I do," I agreed. There was a luncheon at
the inn, fancy, with some awards being given
out. I was supposed to keep an eye on it. I

expected it would also enable me to keep an eye on anyone who might be the mysterious Mr. Davies. Ali might be washing his hands of the investigation; I was not.

The inn was bustling when I made it there mid-morning, fighting bicycles and lanyard-wearers all the way up Commercial Street. Mike was in his office staring at a rather distinctive piece of paper that he whipped out of sight as soon as I entered. "Don't you ever knock anymore? I don't know why I bother having a door."

"If I knocked I wouldn't have seen you hide that paper," I said. "What is it?"

He was flushed. "Nothing."

Oh, good. We were sounding like a mother having a conversation with her kid. Where did you go? *Out.* What did you do? *Nothing.* I wondered, in some distracted part of my brain, if Mirela's Lily would be a sullen teenager someday. Probably. "This isn't," I said to Mike, "a good time for us to start keeping secrets from each other."

"It has nothing to do with you. Or anything else." He opened a drawer, dropped the page in, and slammed it shut. "There. Any other questions?"

I flopped down into his guest chair.
"Tons," I said. "Why do we see the Milky Way
as this discrete thing in the sky, but simultane-
ously we're inside it? I've never understood
that."

He stared at me. "What are you talking
about, Sydney?"

I shrugged. "You asked if I had any other
questions. I have tons of other questions.
More importantly, what's on that paper? Who
wrote you? Is it a love letter?"

"Give it up," he suggested. "Why are you
here?"

"The film society luncheon. Have to make
sure the ducks are all in a row."

"I meant, why are you in my office?"

"Because I care about you and wanted to
see how you are." Well, it was partly true, anyway. "And I want to enlist your help."

"In doing what, exactly?"

"Why do you sound so suspicious?" I
complained. "Can't I just ask a question from
time to time?"

"Sydney." He was fast losing patience.

"Okay," I said, and sighed. "The thing is,
I think whoever killed those people is staying
here at the inn. Or at least had dinner here

night before last." That should get his attention.

It did. "Do you know who it is?"

"I know it's somebody who's not using his real name," I said. "It's complicated, but I think he got out of prison recently and is looking for revenge on Justin Braden."

"Justin Braden wasn't the one killed," said Mike.

"I know. He wanted to put Justin in prison for the murder. He set him up."

"But you're not going to tell me who it is. This guy is running around loose and is maybe a guest in my inn and you're not going to say who it is?"

I leaned forward. "I *don't know*. All I have is a name, and he's really and truly not going to be using it."

Mike was looking thoroughly exasperated. "You have to give me more than that. I need to know if anyone at the Race Point is in any danger," he said. "I have an obligation here."

I was already regretting having said anything to him. "Look. It's a theory, okay? A hypothesis? Justin happened to see someone getting killed years ago and was a witness against this guy in court. We think he's out now and setting Justin up."

252

"That's better," said Mike. "Where was this?" He was pulling his keyboard closer. "When?"

I shrugged. "Ten years ago? Maybe? And it was Boston. The murder was on Comm. Ave."

"There would have been media coverage," said Mike, nodding. "We can see what he looks like. What was the name?"

"Rick Davies," I said, just as the door behind me banged open. "Mike. Need you now," said Glenn.

Mike gave me another look. "We're not finished here," he said.

"I'll wait."

But the moment he was out of the door it was his top drawer, and not the computer, that really interested me. Because I'd seen that paper before, way too stylized, with a drumroll of initials at the top. It had been in Austin Hyde's hand at the meeting we'd had in Glenn's office. And if Austin was sending notes to Mike, I had to see what it said.

***

"Just go for a walk, Sydney," said Ali.

I'd called him the moment I was out of Mike's office. "You don't understand," I said. "I don't trust him. He wants to talk to Mike. He says there's something they need to discuss, and it's in Mike's best interests to meet him. He says he was surprised by how he felt when he saw Mike."

"And?"

"You've seen Austin. Seriously. This isn't someone who's going to come crawling back to his ex. But Mike's vulnerable. Mike probably believes him."

"And it's entirely Mike's business whether he does or not." He was sounding exasperated again.

"If you saw someone running out on the tracks and you knew a train was coming, wouldn't you push them out of the way?"

"Sydney. Listen. You have a luncheon to run. If you have any extra energy, Mike's idea of looking Davies up online is a good one; go do that. Leave Mike alone. And I'm going into a screening right now and I'm turning off my phone."

Damn, but I still wished Austin were the murderer.

I went for a walk. Too many people on the town beaches, so I grabbed the bus that does the beach circuit and jumped off at Beech Forest. It's a small pond with two walking circuits around it; you can do the shorter one in less than half an hour, and it's always calming. You used to be able to feed the chickadees at the start of the circuit; they'd come and perch on your hand with their tiny feet and eat right out of it, but the forest is part of the Cape Cod National Seashore and the rangers won't let you feed any wildlife. But there's so much more here to enjoy: Canada geese, ducks of all sorts, woodpeckers, titmice, blue jays, robins, red-winged blackbirds, osprey, Eastern Phoebes. There's no end to what you can see and hear. I always tell people at the inn to visit the beach, sure, but to spend an afternoon at Beech Forest, too.

And it really does work. By the time I'd come back to the parking area I was breathing better, not quite so obsessed, and ready to do my job again. Wedding and event organizer, that is, and definitely not Girl Detective.

The bus dropped me off at the MacMillan Pier parking lot and I walked back to the inn, trying to keep my sense of joy and wonder at nature as I fought the *human* nature visible on Commercial Street. The sun was out, the air was soft, and I found myself actually smiling at the people with the lanyards. It was the last day of the festival, the closing party (which we blessedly were not hosting, the Crown & Anchor does that) was later in the day, no one else had gotten killed, and Justin wasn't in police custody.

Okay, so we take what we can get.

The dining room looked beautiful, with big black-and-white posters from old Hollywood movies adorning the walls—I immediately looked for my own favorite, *Casablanca*, and don't get me started on everything that's perfect about *Casablanca*—and fresh flowers on every table. Martin the maître d' was tweaking them when I came in. "Everything okay in the kitchen?" I asked.

He knew that was code for *is Adrienne happy?* and answered smoothly enough, "it's fine," in a way that seemed relaxed, so it had to be true. And it was indeed good news. I hadn't wanted to go back and check. I spend a fair bit of my professional time avoiding Adrienne the diva chef.

The awards to be given out were ready, the podium (bedecked with flowers, of course) was ready, presumably the people actually running the show were ready. "Last hurrah of the festival for us," I said to Martin.

He poured a coffee and handed it to me. "Here's to surviving another one!" We clinked cups. The show had very definitely gone on, I thought.

Mike poked his head in. "Is your phone turned off?" he asked me.

"I don't think so." I felt for it in my pocket. "Oh, hell, the ringer's off." I do that accidentally more often than I like to think. "Did you want me?"

"Not me. Ben deRuyter. He called from Whaler's Wharf. Says he has something there you need to see."

"What, now?"

"That's what he said. He's waiting for you, um—" he checked the scrap of paper in his hand "—in the basement. The door's unlocked." He looked at me. "I suppose that makes sense?"

"It does," I said and nodded. Maybe Ben had found something in the basement that showed how Brett's body had been taken from the cinema out to the beach. Maybe he'd examined those tunnels more closely. Maybe the identity of the killer was there—a dropped ring or credit card or something. Ben must have forgotten he'd given me a key. No matter: in three seconds flat, I was back to being

Miss Marple. I looked at Martin. "Do you mind—?"

He waved me away. "Go ahead. We're fine here." And in fact the first luncheon guests had started arriving, chattering and laughing, obviously in good spirits. The show had most definitely gone on. And a year from now they'd say to each other, "Oh, wasn't that the year Brett Falcone was killed? Did they ever figure out what happened? Did they catch the killer?" As though it were merely something they'd read on a news site. The public is fickle.

Mike had already disappeared. I knew better than to call Ali again. I'd meet Ben and see what he had to show me, and then decide what to do. Call Ali, call Julie, call in the troops.

Whaler's Wharf was bustling and busy, the Nut House humming with people getting belated coffees or early ice creams, the shops' wares spilling out onto the pavement. As advertised, the big steel door to the basement was unlocked, and I slipped through it. The light was on and something below me clanged, then was silenced. "Ben!" I called.

"Down here!"

"What did you find?" I was already down the stairs and turning left, toward the tunnel. I took a few steps and looked around me.

Nothing. "Ben?" I called again, making it a question. I suddenly felt very alone.

"Behind you, Sydney."

It wasn't Ben. I'd fallen for the most elementary of ruses, one of the oldest tricks in the book. I turned around slowly, something cold and hard in the pit of my stomach. I already knew who it was. I recognized the voice.

Jack Donnelly, erstwhile film critic and official Nicest Guy In The Room. Agatha Christie had been right, after all: the bad guy turns out to be the one you like the most. "Hello, Jack," I said. This *would* be the first time he got my name right. It hadn't escaped my notice that he was holding a knife in his hand—and blocking my flight back up the stairs. "Or is it Rick?"

"Clever you," he said.

"You did say you'd been away for a while," I pointed out. "And it was just a matter of time before someone looked you up online and saw your face."

"I'll be long gone before that happens," said Jack.

You forget how searingly physical fear is. How it seizes your body and your senses and won't let go. I could feel my heart hammering inside my chest, the blood beating against my eardrums. The coldness in my gut was spreading.

No matter how you looked at it, I was in a cellar alone with a killer, and no one knew I was there.

This time, Ali wouldn't come to the rescue. I spared a brief nostalgic thought for another time when I'd been in danger, up at the top of the Pilgrim Monument, and how Ali had led a charge up the stairs to help. Not this time. Not today. *Breathe, Riley*, I counseled myself. *Breathe. Just breathe.*

Breathing doesn't help you confront murderers, but it's a wise first step in any endeavor.

"A knife," I said. "That's creative. I thought killers stuck to one modus operandi."

"And there you go, reading detective novels again," said Jack sorrowfully. "I'm here to tell you, they're nothing like real life. Go to prison for a few years, that'll teach you what happens in real life."

I shivered. *No, thank you for thinking of me, but no, I think I'll stay away from prison for now.* I was starting to feel a little lightheaded. "Why Caroline?" I asked. Another gem I'd gleaned from the detective novels Jack so easily disparaged: keep them talking while you figure out what to do. This one was on me; I was going to have to use every resource I could, because I was in this alone. "I get why you killed Brett, but why Caroline?" I was trying to be unobtrusive, looking casually around me to see if there could be—what? A weapon? An escape route? The cavalry?

"What is this, Sydney? The final conversation when all is revealed?" Jack still looked pleasant, ordinary, human. I remembered a long-ago conversation with Julie, the first time I'd encountered a murder in P'town, and my realization that evil is, in fact, banal, ordinary. They don't have to look like monsters to be one. "Your perseverance is laudable, but it's not working this time."

"So what?" I demanded. "You kill me, okay, then what happens? I'm not the only one who's figured it out. My boyfriend knows. Justin knows. My manager knows." Something had flickered across his face when I'd used Justin's name: that hatred was still alive and well. Okay, let's go with that. "But that's not even the worst part, is it? Because it was all for nothing. You set Justin up and you kept hammering the police about him and guess what? He's still not going away for any of it. You failed, Jack. An epic failure."

I didn't like the way he was smiling. "Oh, I don't think so," he said. "In fact, he's heading toward the trifecta. Once they find your body, there isn't going to be any more doubt about Justin's guilt."

I hadn't actually thought he was *not* going to kill me, but I'd never before thought of myself as a body. Not exactly what you want to hear from the guy holding the knife in the dimly lit basement. I could be starring in another *Friday the Thirteenth* remake with this backdrop and hackneyed language. Maybe I should just scream and run. That always works out in the horror flicks, doesn't it? *Breathe...*

"I think we'll do it in the tunnel," Jack said. "I wasn't sure, before, but seeing you here, I think that's going to give me the most bang for the buck. I like that white dress. You'll get it dirty going through, but it's going to show up nicely when they open the trap door. And the blood will be very dramatic. I've learned that from watching so many films. Set design. Making sure the audience gets the right visual. It's very important."

I didn't want to dwell on myself as part of a murder set design. Moving along. "Is that how you got Brett outside?" I demanded. "Through the tunnel?"

"I was going to," Jack said, and nodded. It was hard to tell what he was thinking; his expression gave nothing away. "First time I got the key, first time I came down here, I knew I could use the tunnels. Lure him down here same way I got you. Easy as anything."

"But...?" I asked. "You said you were *going* to. So you didn't?"

"He didn't cooperate," said Jack. "Not like you're going to, Sydney. I wanted him to come down here with me. I was going to bring him down and use the knife. I even had the raincoat down here ready."

I must have looked blank. "Raincoat?"

"For blood spatter," he said. "Haven't you learned anything from your amateur efforts?"

I didn't see a raincoat. Maybe he was going to change his mind about me. On the other hand, if he had it here for Brett, he was probably ready to whip it out for me. Maybe I should push it a little instead. No matter what, I wasn't going to die re-enacting the Perils of Pauline. "What do you mean, he wouldn't cooperate?" I asked. "How rude! He didn't just lie down and take it from you! Poor Jack. So what did you have to do? Drag him through all by yourself?"

"You've got to be kidding," he said. "I'm not a mole. Not when there's a big beautiful roof to use that no one can see."

Ben had been spot-on about his selections of the places a murderer would choose, I thought. I'd have to tell him, when I saw him again. *If* I ever saw—no. Don't go there. *Breathe, Riley.* "How did you get him up to the roof?" I asked. "The ladder's steep and partly visible from the film society digs. Dragging him would have been conspicuous."

"Asked him politely," said Jack. There was no mistaking his expression now: he was in full smirk. "Politeness counts. Even in times of stress, you shouldn't forget to be courteous. Of course I didn't drag him anywhere! He was only too happy to come up on the roof along with his brand-new award to pose for photographs for Esquire magazine."

"You don't work for Esquire," I said, pointing out the obvious.

"Oh, dear. Did I neglect telling that to Brett?"

"You're enjoying this, aren't you?"

"Actually, you know, Sydney, I am," he said. "It's kind of surprising. *I'm* totally surprised, anyway. I came to Provincetown to do what I needed to do so I could get on with my life. For retribution—no, no, not that: for *revenge*. Just like the film. What a delicious coincidence that was, by the way."

"I wondered about that," I said.

"But once I got Brett up on that roof, with his award in hand, I felt things I'd never felt before. Completely exhilarated. Like I was on top of the world."

"You took a chance, though," I said. "Anyone from up on top of the Monument could have seen you." Like anyone was watching.

"Not much of a chance," said Jack, as though reading my thoughts. "We went all the way out to the other side, I took all these shots of him posing here and there and I said one final one with the harbor in the background. He was all over it. I pretended to adjust his collar, grabbed the trophy, and as they say in the movies, bada-bing, bada-boom!"

"He didn't notice you wearing gloves," I said. Brett and Justin's prints were the only ones on it.

"Nope. Too full of himself."

"And Justin?"

"Told Brett to text him to meet him out back. Said I didn't want others up on the roof—liability issues, you understand, the insurance company—but I could get a great shot of them together, Justin below and Brett on top. Made sure he didn't mention my name in the text. It was almost too easy."

"And you threw him over the side. And the trophy after him."

"Like I said, it was almost too easy. The guys inside, up in Shirley, they said it was easy, but I never believed them."

"Why not?"

"Duh, Sydney. Because they were inside! Obviously! They got caught. The perfect crime is the crime no one even knows happened. But I'll settle for the second-perfect crime: the one you can hang on someone else."

I couldn't see anything around that could help me. Running seemed to be my only option. Jack was standing between me and the stairs, but I had another alternative besides the tunnel, where he'd surely catch me—I could go for the room with the defunct boiler in it. Slam the door, call for help. As unobtrusively as possible, I started sliding my hand toward my pocket.

Jack was watching. "There's nothing you can do, you know," he said, his voice almost gentle.

"When did I get to be part of your plan?" I asked, and even I could hear the edge of panic running through my voice, feel the desperation. "Why me? I didn't do anything to you."

"You are what I call improvisation, Sydney," said Jack. At least now he seemed to be finally getting my name right. I could have lived without that. "Caroline, too. She saw me getting the key—you know the same key unlocks every door in this building? It's insane. Convenient, but insane. I paid a lot for it, my key, and poor Caroline saw the transaction. I didn't want it coming back to her in hindsight, that image, that memory. And you, my dear— well, I knew from the beginning it would have to be somebody, to cement Justin's guilt. I decided to play it by ear. And I was here when Mr. Whaler's Wharf Owner deRuyter gave you your tour."

"I didn't see you."

"No; I'm pretty unremarkable. Don't get me wrong, I don't mind. It's an asset. Up until then I was thinking it might have to be Irene. I really hoped not. I've grown quite attached to her. So your little tour was music to my ears."

"So glad I could make your visit so successful," I said. The boiler room. It had to be the boiler room. I just had to choose my moment. I yawned, consciously pulling more oxygen into my lungs, into my muscles, and so there, Jack: I learned *that* trick in an Adam Hall thriller. But I still had to choose my moment.

Jack chose it for me. "Okay," he said. "Enough's enough. I have places to go, people to see, and you're what's standing between me and making sure Justin Braden never breathes free air again. He's going to know what I knew. He's going to get beaten up, and worse. He's going to panic, just like I did." He smiled. "I can't wait. Come on now, let's take a walk down the tunnel."

"You can't really expect me to just walk into your knife," I said. I took a deep breath, turned, and ran.

Jack was right behind me; he must have been expecting something. I wasn't going to make it to the boiler room. I wasn't going to—and then I tripped and fell straight out, tripped over some of the debris that had spilled out of one of the storage cages, absurdly enough the kid's sled. I grabbed it and held it out like a shield. I was so desperate it was the only thing I could do; and then there was the most unearthly scream I think I'd ever heard as the sled's blade caught Jack. I couldn't see where or how, just that unbelievable howl, and I threw the sled off me and scuttled backwards, just barely off the floor, out of his reach.

The knife had clattered away from him and he was holding his leg, screaming. He must have launched himself at me to have gotten hurt there. I didn't know if he'd nicked an artery or not, but there was a lot of blood, and he had other things besides murder on his mind. "Help me!"

I was in no mood to get close to him. "Make a tourniquet!" I snarled. I looked around myself, a little desperately—because when it came down to it, I didn't really want to be responsible for Jack bleeding out—and grabbed a sheet from one of the storage cages. It was none too clean, but if wishes were horses… "Here," I said, throwing it to him. "Use this!"

"Get me help!" he howled. "I don't want to die!"

I didn't want him to, either, but I had no idea how strong he was going to feel once his leg was in better shape. I looked around again, remembering the padlocks hanging open. "Walk over there," I said, pointing.

"What? No!"

"Then I'm not calling for help. I'm leaving you to die here alone. Or get arrested, whichever your leg allows. Walk over there."

It was more of a hobble, but he managed. I swung the door closed behind him and snicked the padlock into place. Heaven only knew where that key was. He was still working on his tourniquet when I turned to go. "Sydney!"

"What is it?" My heartrate was just finally coming down to normal.

"I like you, you know. I didn't want to have to kill you. It just worked out that way."

"Yeah," I said. "I'll try to remember that."

16

I got up to the ground floor, made it through the door, shut it behind me, and came absurdly close to falling again, my knees were shaking so much. Here's one thing I've learned: no matter how often your life is in danger, it never doesn't feel like the first time.

Actually, I wanted to throw up.

My hands were shaking as I pulled the phone from my pocket and located Ali's icon. *Answer, please answer, please answer...*

"*Cara!* Where are you?"

"At Whaler's Wharf," I managed to say. My throat seemed to be squeezing shut on me, too. "Ali, it's Jack..."

"I know," he said. "We found the trial reports, and Ellie said it was the same guy she'd seen following her. But—"

"Listen," I interrupted. "He's here. He…"

"The important thing," Ali interrupted in turn, "is are you all right? I've been calling and calling."

And my ringer was off. "I'm okay," I said. "But Jack—Ali, I've got Jack in a cage."

There was a pause, as he was no doubt asking himself if he'd heard correctly. "*Cara?*" he asked, a little doubtfully.

Relief was washing over me. "It's okay, just come over, okay? And bring Julie or somebody. Oh, and the EMTs, too. I think he's hurt."

"Then you can check on Mike," he said. "He's gone over to Ross' Grill. He's meeting Austin."

"What!"

"Yeah, but I have some concerns. I didn't know you were there, too." There was a pause. "Austin has a handgun registered under his name," he said.

"No," I said. "Can't be. He couldn't have flown with it—"

"—except in his luggage," said Ali. "Anyway, the police will be heading over. I just realized what was going on a few minutes ago. And I—"

"Sorry, Ali," I said. "Gotta go." And then I was running up the stairs to the second floor, running down the balcony that fronted the offices and studios, running around the rotunda with the fountain gurgling and sparkling below me, my legs finding strength they hadn't had five minutes before.

Jerking open the glass front doors, running into the bar, the dining area, looking wildly around. *Mike, just be okay, Mike, please be all right...*

He wasn't there. Austin wasn't there. I was nearly out on the deck when I heard the scream from outside.

I stopped myself at the railing. Below me, right where Brett's body had landed when Jack hefted it off the roof, were Mike and Austin. And Austin had the gun out.

I don't think I gave it a second's thought. The adrenaline that had faded slightly from the cellar had kicked in again—I could taste it in my mouth, bitter and metallic—and before anyone could say anything I grabbed a chair, jumped up on it, and went over the railing, landing squarely on both Austin and my left arm. Pain flooded my senses, red and sizzling and agonizing. I was aware of people around me, milling, Austin being removed from my grasp, Mike's voice coming from a long distance away, but all I felt was pain. Literally breathtaking pain.

A scene worthy, I thought, of the Provincetown Theater of old.

***

On Monday, the film festival over (and, as far as I was concerned, dead and buried), I was sitting in the dining room at the Race Point Inn, my arm in a sling given to me by the emergency room doctor, and my very strong painkillers at my side. I was only permitted to take one every four hours.

I was counting the *minutes*.

Ali set my coffee in front of me and sat down. He'd extended his time off so he could take me to Cape Cod Hospital where, tomorrow, an osteopathic surgeon was going to reunite the pieces of my shattered bone with each other. It couldn't happen too soon from my point of view.

"I never knew it would hurt so much," I said. I'd been saying the same thing for the past three hours.

"You've been lucky to never break a bone before, *cara*," said Ali. He'd been saying that a lot, too.

"I had no idea how lucky," I said fervently.

"At least," he said, "you did it spectacularly. I broke my arm once on my own kitchen floor. You saved Mike's life."

I had done that, it appeared. Austin Hyde had apparently mooned over Mike for years, and had come to Provincetown determined to either get him back—or make sure no one else would ever have him. Mike had offered him the latter option.

Jack—or Rick, as I suppose was correct—had also enjoyed a trip to the hospital; I'd even seen him, in passing, in the big emergency room in Hyannis, our ambulances having left Provincetown at about the same time. He had uniformed policemen with him, though; I had a ragtag assortment of Mike, Ali, Glenn, and—for some reason I never quite grasped—Ellie. Rick's next stop was the jail in Bourne; me, they sent home with painkillers that didn't actually kill the pain. Now I understood what people meant when they talked about drugs taking the edge off. I could have done with a bigger edge, to tell the truth.

Justin had left after giving me an awkward little speech that was half apology and half thanks. I wished him well, though with a family like his I suspected he still had some rough times ahead. All that and grieving, too.

Ali's phone beeped and he looked at the screen, smiling. "We're in here!" he called out loudly just as Mike came into the room.

With Mirela.

With a baby.

I stared at them, and turned to say something to Ali, who was still scrolling through texts on his phone. "Oh, no."

"What?" I demanded.

He looked up. "You didn't promise your mother an *autograph*, did you?" he asked.

Author's Note

I've taken a couple of small liberties with the layout of Whaler's Wharf, notably where the "Provincetown Theater" stones are out back; in my mind (and story) I've removed an inconvenient rack of kayaks and moved the stones closer to the building so that bodies can be deposited (or land) there more efficiently.

And the story of the key is true—up until very recently, nearly everyone who'd ever worked at the Wharf (and anyone who *knew* anybody who'd ever worked at the Wharf) had a copy and could access just about everything in the building. But don't go trying it out— Ben deRuyter (yes, he's a real person) had the building re-keyed not long after I wrote this book. I'm sure there was no connection.

As always, many of the people in this story are real; you never know when you'll be visiting P'town and will run into one of them. I'm grateful to everyone who helps give Sydney interesting places and people to explore.

Acknowledgments

So many people help, inspire, and shepherd a book from the first idea to the printed page. As always, first, last, and foremost, I must thank Arthur Mahoney of HomePort Press. Sydney belongs to him as much as she does to me. He is a friend, colleague, guru, and all-around delight. I wish every author had an Arthur Mahoney in her life.

My thanks go as always to all the beautiful people of Provincetown, who generously allow me to use so many of their own special selves in my books. Any errors in their portrayal are mine.

To those who contribute in myriad ways to the creation of a Sydney story: Colin Kegler, Pat Medina, Susan Blood, Ann Robinson, Amanda Robinson, Chip Capelli (who hasn't missed a single event—you finally made it into one of the stories!), Michael Ponestowski, Fred Biddle, Carem Bennett, Dianne Kopser, Michelle Crone (whose wedding planning inspires Sydney), Bob Allen, Julie & Katy Blackburn, Lady Di, and Tony, Suzanne, and Albert Rodrigues. Special thanks to Ben deRuyter, who really does own Whaler's Wharf and who really did suggest how to get a body from one end of it to the other. Thank you to Mike Tullio for helping me understand detectives (as if!), to my beautiful family Anastasia and Sydnia Czarnecki; and to Sister Kathryn, for always pointing me in the right direction.

Thanks to Deborah Karacozian, Nan Cinnater, and Clayton Nottleman for so energetically being my emissaries at the Provincetown Bookshop, to Jeff Peters and East End Books, and to Miladinka Milic for Sydney's amazing cover designs. And to Kyre Song, who is so much more than just my web guy.

Thank you to all the people who make the Provincetown International Film Festival the consistently amazing experience and success it is.

Thanks to Erin Delaney for her peerless editing, and to my wonderful First Readers: Kimberlee Sams, Corinne Diana, Margo Nash, and A.C. Burch. Any mistakes that remain here are mine, not theirs. To the ladies from Jungle Red Writers for their support and inspiration. And to the New England chapter of the Sisters in Crime—well, for sisterhood!.

My gratitude goes out to you all, to all of my beautiful Provincetown, and to anyone I might have inadvertently left out—for sometimes I am a bear of very little brain.

No, not that kind of bear.

About The Author

Jeannette de Beauvoir writes mystery and historical fiction (and often books at the intersection of the two) that uncover dark secrets and hidden truths, and explore a sense of connection to place.

A Book Sense Book-of-the-Year finalist, she's a member of the Authors Guild, the Mystery Writers of America, Sisters in Crime, and the National Writers Union.

Her delight is to find characters true to the spaces in which they live. She herself lives and writes in a cottage in Provincetown, on Cape Cod, Massachusetts, and loves the collection of people who assemble at a place like Land's End.

Find out more, and read her blog, at **jeannettedebeauvoir.com**.

Did You Enjoy This Book?

If you did, please…

1) **share your opinion** on Goodreads and/or Amazon;

2) **visit my Amazon page** and check out some of my other books;

3) give the book a boost; **tell people about** it on Facebook and Twitter;

4) **subscribe to my newsletter** at **jeannettedebeauvoir.com** for book reviews, short stories, quizzes, free stuff, previews of upcoming work, and more;

5) ask your local bookseller **to stock** Sydney Riley books;

6) make them your **choice for your next book club** meeting (I'll even join you by Skype or Zoom if you'd like me to!);

7) **email me** at jeannettedebeauvoir@gmail.com;

8) and **watch for** the next Sydney Riley mystery from Homeport Press!